SIN WALKS INTO THE DESERT

This is a work of fiction. All characters and events are products of the author's imagination. Any resemblance to anyone, living or dead, is purely coincidental.

Author's photo by Chris Sessions Photography
ChrisSessionsPhotography.com

© 2014 Matt Ingwalson
ISBN-13: 978-1497343405
ISBN-10: 1497343402

4

CHAPTER ONE: ARIZONA, 2011

Sin spent an hour watching videos on the Internet and another hour cleaning a pistol that didn't need cleaning.

When he finished he sat on his old green couch, staring at the walls and the window, the room gone dark around him. The pistol wasn't even a pistol anymore. It was just the thing his hand would've felt empty without.

He sat there, eyes focused on nothing much, racking the slide and dropping the hammer. Racking the slide and dropping the hammer. Racking the slide and four stage drawing – clear leather, turn the weapon towards the threat, bring your hands together in front of your heart, extend towards the threat as you start pulling the trigger.

He was twenty-two and he had some dim awareness he was supposed to be on a date or at a concert or, failing all those things, at a bar doing shots and making loud cheering noises with a wild group of friends.

Finally the boredom got to be too much. Sin didn't need more tattoos, but there were people at a parlor up in Tucson who knew him by name and he had nowhere else to go.

He started to undo his jeans to clip on his concealed carry holster but then decided, fuck it. He laid the pistol in a drawer, grabbed his bus pass, and headed for the door.

In the hallway he stopped, extended one foot backwards, caught the door before it latched shut. Something didn't feel right. His eyes flashed up and down the rows of doors, registered ceiling lights that had blown out and corners with indistinct shadows behind them. Nothing out of the ordinary, really.

Sin went back inside and opened up the drawer.

El Viejo had Berettas so Sin'd wanted a Beretta. But el Viejo's were M9s, classic military sidearms chambered for 9, so Sin asked for the new model, the Px4 with a rail on it and the smooth black slide, rounded and mean, space age almost. And Sin wanted it chambered in .40, not 9. DA/SA please, with the exposed hammer. And fullsize even though he intended to carry it tucked inside skinny jeans because fuck that compact shit. El Viejo'd given him that and also a custom-molded leather IWB holster for it.

It was about the best gift ever.

Sin clipped the holster inside his jeans, brass checked the gun and seated it. He tugged his t-shirt down. It pretty much covered his belt and even if he leaned the wrong way, what was anybody going to say? This was Arizona, after all.

Sin stepped out of his tiny rented hole-in-the-wall apartment and thought, "I didn't grab a spare clip." And then he thought, "Fuck it. For real this time."

He let the door latch behind him and went off into the night.

Sindy was the name of the tattoo artist who did the roses, the kanji characters, and even some Apache stuff.

Lots of people thought it would be cool if her and Sin hooked up, just based on their names. Sin thought it would be OK too, and so did Sindy. So at an apartment party once they went ahead and did it. They left the rest of the crowd playing drinking games and found an empty bedroom, kissed for a couple minutes, and had sex as competently as their drunken bodies would let them. It was more awkward and sloppy than hot and sexy, but it was still the closest thing to a relationship Sin'd ever had.

When Sin walked into the parlor, he and Sindy made eye contact. She cocked her head to one side, letting her bleached-out hair swing over the teardrop she had tattooed on her right cheek, and Sin saw one corner of her mouth come up, a tiny smile.

Sindy was almost done putting a diamond tiara on a pretty blonde ASU student's pelvis. The girl was holding her sorority t-shirt up over her chest with one hand and had the fingernails of the other dug deep into the table. She was gritting her teeth and she kept making little mewing noises.

Virgin.

The pretty blonde had a pretty brunette friend who must've gotten something she was going to regret too, because she was off lying on one of the red vinyl couches with a hand gingerly pressing a bandage onto her bellybutton. She was staring at the ceiling with big watery eyes, probably drunk as hell.

Sin sat his ass down on the couch next to the brunette. She said, "What's up?" Sin shrugged and pulled out his phone.

This was a girl who wasn't used to guys blowing her off. Then again, none of the guys she knew at ASU had hand tattoos. She went back to staring at the ceiling, wondering when it started spinning, trying to figure out if the ache in her midsection was the tribal ring around her bellybutton or Jell-O shots on their way back up.

Sin started scrolling through drawings of desert things. Constellations and cactuses, coyotes and kingsnakes. He'd planned to stop with the ink after they completed his forearm sleeves, but a month or so ago he'd been sitting around and Sindy had been bored so he'd let her put an Apache tomahawk across his shoulder and now it seemed like no big deal to keep going.

El Viejo had once told him, "Don't get a tattoo anywhere a judge can see it, my boy."

Sin'd held up his middle finger, displaying the tree roots that trailed down to his fingernails. "Judge see this, el Viejo?"

A couple of other artists were hanging out putting ink on drunk kids, the only species who wanted to get tattooed at midnight on a weekend. A guy Sin didn't know was getting his ears stretched.

One by one, people acknowledged Sin with a nod or a wave. Mostly everybody stayed cool, listened to indie rock on the speakers, drank water.

Sindy rubbed Aquaphor over the college

girl's pelvis and said, "Just relax, princess. I'll get you a bandage and the aftercare card, you and your girlfriend can get back out to your scene."

She came over to Sin, reached down and picked up the brunette girl's legs and flopped down on the couch. The brunette moaned and nestled her feet back down onto Sindy's lap, which seemed fine with everyone involved.

Sindy leaned into Sin, kissed him behind his ear where his black hair was shaved up away from the neckline. "Ink or a drink tonight?" she said. "I've almost made my dime."

Sin shrugged, happiest when things were quiet, not really dying to go anywhere except where he was.

That was when he got the text from la Calavera. It read, "We must talk."

Sindy looked over Sin's shoulder at his screen. "Who talks?" she said.

He shrugged and tapped the call button.

The voice on the other end of the phone sounded like sandpaper would sound if it whispered and was a woman. Every other word, she had to pause and breathe, shallow breaths that took forever to happen. Sin was used to it, waited patiently for her to get the words out. "Thanks." Wait. "For calling." Wait. "Kiddo."

To which Sin said nothing.

"Seen el Viejo recently?"

"About a week." When Sin spoke, it was at some volume just barely above silent. Catrina waited a bit to make sure he'd actually finished before she went on.

"Not since he went to the place?"

"No."

"He's AWOL."

"No, he's at that Denzhone place for a few days still."

"He's got a situation."

Anybody else, Sin would've laughed. El Viejo didn't have situations, except the arthritis that kept him in his rocking chair and off the streets where he belonged. But the voice on the other end of the phone, the voice that talked instead of texted, it belonged to la Calavera. Catrina Limon. Special Agent Catrina Limon.

Special Agent is one of those titles like Senator. Once you have it, you get to keep it forever.

El Viejo'd met Catrina when she moved out to do border security with the ATF many years ago. He'd consulted with her unit on strategy, tactics and local customs, and eventually they got around to pulling triggers.

Anybody el Viejo pulled triggers with didn't screw around much.

That went double for la Calavera, even if she, like el Viejo, was stuck in a chair these days. She was one of the first and best female agents the federal government ever had training anti-terrorist units along the Mexican border. She was old even then, older than el Viejo, but they both had family in the same area of Wyoming so they shared that in common. Or maybe el Viejo fell in love with the idea of an elderly female out in the desert commanding a tactical team. He'd taken her under his wing, taken her drinking, taken her out to the desert to show her how the cartels set up mobile staging sites to get guns, drugs, workers and slaves across the border.

Turned out she'd chalked up three kills as a

sniper back in her time someplace she couldn't really talk about or maybe didn't want to. Nicaragua? Cambodia? She wouldn't say. But three. No shit. Most guys couldn't say that, could they?

El Viejo could say it a few times over, but he was a different topic altogether.

"Why do you say that?" Sin said.

"We got." Wait. "A photo."

"OK," he said and he hung up his phone. No need to be polite or say goodbye. You couldn't offend someone like la Calavera.

Sin stood up and slipped his phone back in his pocket.

Even though it was just about fall, it was still seventy degrees at night and he had no jacket. He shook his shoulders a bit and let his t-shirt arrange itself over his belt.

"You going?" Sindy asked.

He nodded.

"You coming back?"

Sin didn't know how to say goodbye, especially since he'd just got there. Finally he leaned down and kissed Sindy where she'd kissed him, on the skin up underneath her ear. She had a little rose there that trailed down the back of her neck, the stem ending somewhere near her spine.

He didn't really make eye contact with her as he slouched towards the door.

It was a thing, getting to Catrina and Petr. They lived all the way down in Green Valley and it took a bit of planning and a long, dark ride on a Sun Tran bus, Sin staring out the window, not seeing much but the silhouettes of mesas out there in the black Arizona desert. By the time the bus let him off on a side street along nineteen, there was a thin white line throbbing at the edge of the eastern horizon and the sky above it was starting to go navy.

There was a coffeeshop a couple blocks away. Good thing. Sin walked in, got a box to go, crossed over La Canada and started hiking up a winding street, past a white stone sign with the name of a retirement community on it. By the time he crested the hill, the navy'd rolled west and the east was a pure and pale blue.

Catrina and Petr's home was way toward the back of the community and mostly it was like any other place around. One story, so there were no stairs for the old folks to trip down. Sliding screen doors, to keep out poisonous desert things. A flat back porch with a low fence the neighbors could see over, so no one could have a stroke and lie out there alone, baking to death in the summer sun.

Their alarm system was a little better than their neighbors. That was all.

Sin knocked at the door and waited for a long time because it takes old folks a long time to do anything, and Petr and Catrina were the type of people you probably didn't want to walk in on unannounced. They still had their weapons around somewhere and they had a lot of them. So Sin stood on the five-foot-square front porch and stayed still, his black t-shirt and jeans blending with the long shadows.

Finally Petr swung the door open. He was a very old man, tall and painfully thin. Even though it was early, he wore long twill pants and a newsboy cap. He spoke only Swedish, so he simply smiled and turned. Sin followed.

The home had just three rooms: a bedroom, a bathroom, and a living space with a little kitchenette in the corner.

All three rooms were filled with plants, dozens of them, big wide-leafed green things pumping out oxygen for Catrina's remaining half a lung. The plants made the home feel fresh and almost humid, especially coming in out of the dry early morning air.

She sat in her wheelchair, a blanket over her knees, both hands curled up underneath it in her lap. Her hair had gone white and it'd got so thin you could see her scalp wrinkled beneath, but she'd taken the time to put it up in a bun on top of her head anyway. She had on a white cotton shirt, collar, buttons buttoned up tight around her neck.

Petr came around and stood behind her and he smiled and made a Swedish sound, like he was happy to see Sin again after a couple months. But Catrina was a sterner sort of human and she wasn't brooking any small talk.

"You brought coffee. Do you need a cup?"

she asked.

Sin nodded.

"Help yourself. Then sit."

Sin did as he was instructed, searching the cabinets for a mug with a rim that wasn't too chipped up. Finally he found one. He poured the coffee into it, drank half the cup down, refilled it, and went to crouch on the floor next to Catrina's ankles, squatting like the Apaches squatted in their moccasins, keeping their skin off the scalding sand.

He looked up past her wrinkled face right into her grim blue eyes and asked, "What you got?"

Without looking at her husband, Catrina said, "Ge honom fotot," and Petr reached one hand out past her shoulders. His fist had thick blue veins tunneling all across it, as brightly colored, in their own way, as the tattoos on Sin's hands. In the man's knobby old fingers there was a photo.

Sin took it. It showed a giant sitting by a firepit on a smooth stone patio. The fire threw just enough light to warm the side of his face and silhouette a worn cowboy hat. In the foreground of the photo, a hundred yards of black dirt and scrub.

Behind the man, sliding glass doors giving back the firelight tenfold. Above the flat roof of the condo was the moon, round and white as a flying saucer.

Sin looked at la Calavera and said, "Moon was like this a couple nights ago."

The old lady nodded. Her eyes flicked outside her patio doors and then back down to Sin.

Sin flipped the photo over. Back was blank.

"We called..." Wait. Breathe, Catrina, breathe. "Denzhone." It went on like that, word after word, the old lady having to stop and work to get air into her lung. Over time, she got the words out. "They say he checked in, but they couldn't find him."

"It come in an envelope?"

La Calavera nodded. But then she shook her head no. Yes, it came in an envelope. No, there weren't any fingerprints.

"Postmark?"

Catrina looked out the sliding doors of the condo again, out onto her own deck. She said, "North of Tucson."

"Got a theory?"

Catrina shook her head. Sin looked up at Petr

and he, too, shook his head.

The woman said, "We'd hoped he had told you something. If not..." Here she paused, not just to get back some air, but to look pointedly at Sin. When he shook his head, she went on. "Something has happened."

Sin looked like he didn't give a fuck about anything, but he did. El Viejo'd saved his life. He took a second to think. "What it looks like, someone stalking an agent, you got to call the bureau, right?"

She nodded a bit. "If el Viejo is in danger, we thought you should know."

Now Sin rose up from his crouch and squinted out the glass doors, looked for places someone could be hiding with a camera, a rifle, a scope. "Someone sent you this for some reason. You going to be ok, la Calavera?"

Catrina made a tiny movement with her hands under the blanket. Sin could make out an outline down there, the barrel of a snubby. Most likely a .38 Special, but better to hit with a .38 than miss with a .45, right?

Sin smirked. The old lady smirked right back.

He put the photo in his pocket and headed for the door.

For a moment, Sin couldn't bear the thought of the bus ride back. "Maybe just run it," he thought. What had it been, forty minutes down once they reached nineteen? He looked up the highway, straight shot of asphalt up north to Tucson. Nothing except Indian casinos and gas stations. Stupid idea. Sun was out. He'd waste all day and get a burn. He walked to the stop and waited for SunTran like a normal person.

The whole ride back, Sin kept standing up and stretching out his knee. The last time el Viejo and he went hunting for bad guys, he'd had it kicked in by a mobster in from NYC. Most days, the knee felt fine, but if he sat too long, he'd have to stretch it out.

Ever since, Sin watched el Viejo and he saw how hard it was for the old man to even get around anymore and thought, "That's going to be me." Not in a good way or a bad way exactly. Just a statement of fact. People who make whole lives tracking down bad guys die with scars.

El Viejo'd been a marine sniper, an FBI instructor, and finally a private eye hunting the desert for whoever people would pay him to hunt. Cheating husbands, runaway daughters, missing immigrants. Sometimes he'd get hired to run security for a concert or something. For two decades el Viejo could do it all and then one day he couldn't. The arthritis made it hard for him to move and the diabetes kept him on a strict diet of broccoli and insulin. He'd had to fold up shop.

Hence Denzhone.

Luxury condos with marble floors and Egyptian cotton sheets, big firepits out back. All organic, all natural. Women with no hair, on the comeback trail from chemo. Middle-aged men hiding out for a weekend with their mistresses. Trust fund hippies trying to get in touch with their chakras and shit. It was a luxury vacation spa and a spiritual retreat, with the scorpions and the snakes and the ghosts of the Apache hiding in the brush.

A few years back, el Viejo'd helped the guy who owned Denzhone track down some Aztec artifacts that'd been stolen from a gallery at the resort. So when the doctor said, "Harrison, you need to go somewhere quiet. Try some yoga, get a massage, maybe write down all the adventures you've had in your life," el Viejo rang the guy up and asked him a favor.

When he told Sin where he was heading, Sin looked up Denzhone on his phone and said, "You're going to hate it, el Viejo."

The old man had laughed his big barrel laugh and clapped Sin on the shoulder. He said, "My boy, even the Spartans took time to wash their weapons. Perhaps some peaceful evenings of reflection truly are in order."

Sin'd rolled his eyes.

Sin walked the three miles from the bus stop to where el Viejo lived. It was hot as hell and he hadn't showered or even really slept in a couple days, and the walk didn't make him feel any better.

On the way, he texted the firing range where he watched the front desk and the concert venue where he worked security and told them both he needed a couple days off, something came up. Weird things come up in the lives of people who work for an hourly wage at places like firing ranges and concert venues. Nobody asked Sin questions. Just texts back. "K. See u next week." "Whatever dude."

El Viejo's house was the standard southwest stucco thing, small and unassuming in a suburb outside Tucson. Sin stood on the front porch for about a minute, ringing the bell, not expecting anything to happen, but wanting to be sure before he just went barging in.

Then he went through the gate to the back, smashed the glass on the sliding door off the patio, reached through and let himself in.

The house wasn't booby trapped or even alarmed. El Viejo was his own home defense system. There was a stainless steel custom 1911 with a four and a quarter inch barrel hidden between the couch cushions, cocked and locked. A no-hassle, never-fail, bet-your-life Ruger .357 in a go-bag on his bedpost. These days he kept the M9s under the drivers seats of his Cadillac and his minivan.

Sin walked across the tile floor of the kitchen and down the hallway, staying slightly to one side, but not right along the wall. He moved carefully, taking time in every room, getting it right, staying alive.

He approached the corners and the doorways methodically, starting near the wall and then taking little half steps out and around them, scanning floor to ceiling, taking another little step, scanning again, making sure he was clear before he exposed his body, getting out of the funnels and into the rooms.

He did these things by instinct seared in by repetition. He'd cleared this house before with el Viejo behind him, telling him what he was doing right and wrong the whole way.

"Don't put your weapon into the hallway before your eyes, son. It could be snatched away from you."

"Don't enter on the hinge side of the door, give yourself every opportunity to see your adversary before he sees you."

"Darkness is your friend. Find the darkest shadow in the room and stay in it as long as you can.

Stay a predator, no matter how hard they try to make you prey."

How old had Sin been? Fourteen? Fifteen? Seemed like a long while ago.

El Viejo's bedroom. A single bed, a simple dresser. But everything was custom-built, hardwood furniture. Sin felt real weird being in there. He tried to go through the room looking for clues, but he found nothing really, and he didn't want to dig too deep, although he knew el Viejo would tell him he should. A toothbrush and a suitcase were missing, but everything else seemed OK. There was nothing to indicate the old man didn't intend to come back.

Sin opened the door to the garage. The Cadillac was gone but the minivan was there, and the keys were hanging on the hook by the door.

Sin went down wooden steps to the basement and got the M40, the rifle el Viejo had taken with him from the Marines to the FBI. It hadn't been loaded in years, but the old man kept it up and it was a thing of beauty, all polished wood and bolt action.

Sin'd trained with the rifle before, years ago, back when el Viejo was beating the criminal out of him, forcing him to run barefoot in the desert and shoot coyotes sniper-style, making fires and sleeping under the stars for weeks on end.

He put it in the back of the minivan with a box of cartridges and arranged some blankets over them.

He went back into the house and grabbed the go-bag with the flashlight, the first aid kit, the pocketknife, the bet-your-life gun, the solar blanket, the boonie hat, all the stuff you never needed until you needed it right away. He put that on the passengers seat.

Then he took the M9 from under the drivers seat, went into the TV room, and swapped it with el Viejo's 1911 Commander.

He sat down and took a little extra time holding that weapon. It was just so beautiful, felt so right. The way the beavertail slipped back over the webbing between his thumb and finger when his grip was high, it felt like a little orgasm in his hand, honest to god. The only thing that'd ever come close was his Px4, and even that wasn't quite so satisfying; its long first trigger pull couldn't match the snappy single action and the big bang of the .45s going off.

Like a goddamn orgasm.

On the way out the door, Sin grabbed the 1911's IWB holster and a couple boxes of .45s.

He paused to wonder where el Viejo's shotgun was, the Remington 870. But no, fuck it. Maybe the old man had it in the trunk of the Cadillac or something. He must've taken some weapon with him, even if he was going to a luxury spa in the middle of the desert.

And of course, the old man never went anywhere without his cane, and he could do a lot of damage with that.

Sin stood by the open door of the minivan and checked the status of every weapon, racking every slide, chambering rounds.

Inside the garage, the guns' wonderful noises were amplified. The magazines echoed like horse hooves in a canyon. Every snapping safety clapped gleefully off. And when Sin slammed the slides shut, oh man, it sounded like god himself had swung his sledge.

Then Sin started the minivan's motor,

wheeled out of the garage, and drove north, out the other end of Tucson, into the desert.

Sin woke up in the back of the minivan, spooning the hardshell case that held the M40. It was dark. He stayed perfectly still and listened for movement, for rustling, for voices.

Nothing.

Slowly he pressed his body away from the floor and peeked out the window.

Again, nothing.

Sin hit the light on his mil spec watch. It was two in the morning.

He'd gotten dinner at a fast food restaurant and when he pulled back onto the highway, he'd noticed his eyes wouldn't focus on the road anymore. He'd taken the exit towards Denzhone for about twenty minutes and then pulled over into a gas station parking lot, crawled in back and fallen asleep.

Six hours in an exposed location. El Viejo would have smacked him.

According to his phone, Denzhone was only

about five more miles up the road.

Sin took the Px4 from the floor of the minivan and clipped it back inside his jeans. He shoved his phone, keys, wallet and a windbreaker into the go-bag and slung it over his shoulder. Then he got out of the minivan, set the alarm, and looked back in through the windows, making sure everything lethal was covered up or tucked under the seats.

He shoved his hands into his pockets and started walking.

The moon was up and this far north of Tucson there weren't any city lights to blur it out. Sin could make out the ridge of the Santa Catalinas in the distance. Between the road and the point where the mountains started to climb, the brush was dense, dead and dry, five feet tall with just an occasional oak or saguaro poking above it.

Sin walked as silently as humans can, but he knew that in the brush there were things even quieter. Horned owls, ground squirrels, coyotes, all sorts of snakes – rattlers and kings.

After half an hour he passed a spot where a patch of dirt and pebbles extended into the scrub. He walked into it and squatted down, squinting, trying to see things that did not wish to be seen. He slowed his breath and stayed as motionless as an owl on a branch, but whatever was in there was even stiller than he.

Sin picked up a stone and arched it high, twenty feet up and twenty feet out into the brush. He heard it rustle and then plink dully on the dirt. Nothing scattered. Nothing slithered. Nothing took flight into the night sky.

Slowly Sin stood, backed up onto the road, and walked on. There weren't any more exits between him and Denzhone anymore. Just a few miles of two-lane blacktop.

CHAPTER TWO: WYOMING, 1999

Anderson Kenfax sat on his sister's bed and wondered why she'd abandoned him.

"You're going to miss the bus."

Missing the bus was a major deal. It was a long thirty minutes to school, more when the rain or the snow came to the high plains. His mom was working a job at the local hospital, didn't have time to drive him to school. His dad was out hunting the next couple days in the sense that he and his buddies were drinking cans of light beer, tossing them in the back of a pickup truck, waiting for the deer to come down to the lake at dusk, popping them, and putting them in the back of the truck with the cans.

Anderson really couldn't miss the bus without creating a big hassle for everyone.

"Seriously Anderson, we have to go."

Still he didn't move.

Nicki's bed hadn't been slept in for months. Her boyfriend had graduated, gone to State to play ball. When she got out the next year, everybody assumed she'd follow. Instead she'd left them all behind, moved to New York City with some guy none of them ever heard of before. Sometimes they got phone calls that carried strange little details about her life, the theater school kids she ran with, some hint of whose couch she was crashing on. More often, they'd pick up the phone and Nicki would just start in on them, tirades about anarchy, vegetarianism and art. The Destiny Of The People. Some newsletter she was trying to publish, *Chaos Theory*. It didn't sound romantic or dangerous. It sounded fucking stupid and Anderson missed his big sister.

"Anderson! Please!"

Thirty minutes on the bus. Thirty minutes of hell. But it would all be different soon. It had to be. Anderson couldn't go on like this.

That morning had been the first time he'd ever touched a firearm other than the Kenfax gopher gun. Anderson's dad didn't realize his boy knew there was a loaded .357 on the top shelf of the bedroom closet.

Now it was Dad didn't know where it was.

Anderson picked up his backpack.

"I'm coming."

Thirty minutes on the bus. Thirty minutes of pussy this and faggot that. Thirty minutes of three cowboy assholes spitting at him and flicking his ears.

Stupid baseball hats and cowboy boots. Who wears a fucking baseball hat with cowboy boots? Asshole seventeen-year-old hick motherfuckers, that's who. Didn't these guys have a fucking truck they could drive to school so they could just leave him in peace?

But getting called names was nothing. Just Anderson's daily grind. There'd been worse.

Like when he'd been punched in the back of the head so hard he couldn't barely see to get off the bus and the bus driver had screamed at him, "You high? You high on my bus?" And she'd slapped him on the head as he'd gotten off too, just for good measure, thinking you had to teach these teenage rebel kids their place.

One time, one of the cowboys grabbed him by his long hair and forced him to the ground, made him kiss his boot, asked Anderson if deathcore faggots liked to give head or take it up the ass.

Anderson was eleven and twelve years old.

And even all that wouldn't have been so bad except the girls on the bus, they'd watched it happen. Yeah, they'd rolled their eyes, told the cowboys cut it out and leave the little kid alone. But Anderson knew those pretty girls would never go out with the skinny kid, the loser, the wimp who got his face shoved in the floor. Sure the girls might tell the cowboys to stop it while they were on the bus. But after school, they'd still walk home together and hang out together and together they'd go do whatever it was seventeen-year-old girls did with seventeen-year-old boys. That killed something inside Anderson. It hurt so bad for some reason his eleven-year-old brain didn't understand.

But today Anderson had the gun in his backpack. So when someone flipped him off or spit at him, he just thought about that weight, the cylinder with the bullets inside, and it made everything OK.

Anderson got off the bus, started walking up the sidewalk to school, head down, not making eye contact, trying to make sure his old black tennis shoes didn't slip on the frost that had formed overnight.

Almost to the stairs, he felt a boot in the small of his back. He started to fall, but he couldn't take his hand off his backpack's straps, not with what he was carrying in there. So Anderson went down face first, cheek scraping on the wet ice and the cold concrete.

He didn't even see who'd done it. The

cowboys and the crowd passed him by like cows in a stampede. Run at your own risk. Fall and you catch hooves. Nobody's fault but your own.

The school bell rang.

As he picked himself off the cement, Anderson felt again how his backpack was heavier today than most days and it filled him with pride, warmed his chest, made the blood on his cheek seem like a war wound, instead of just another sign that he was a fucking pussy too small and too skinny to fight back.

He cast his eyes up at the sunrise and saw a hawk up there, high in the sky. It wasn't big and it was so far away, but Anderson could tell it was a hawk by the way it kept its wings open, saved its strength, coasted on the November winds that were sweeping across the high plains, looking down at the ground, waiting patiently for a rabbit or a gopher or even a snake.

Anderson's cheek bled and his shoulder hurt from where he'd bounced off the concrete and even his lower back hurt because of how the corners of his textbooks dug into his spine. None of it mattered to him. It didn't have to be this way much longer. As long as he had the gun in his backpack, it was his decision when to end it all.

There were only two schools around, the k-through-five and the six-through-senior. And the bullying had started the first day of sixth grade.

When Nicki'd left, she'd gifted her baby brother a bunch of albums and books he didn't understand but loved all the same. Misfits and Black Flag. *Catcher In The Rye* and *See A Grown Man Cry*.

Anderson didn't have a friend to sit with on the bus, so on that first day of big kids' school, he'd kept his eyes down, his nose in one of his sister's books.

They were on one of the long stretches of pencil-thin blacktop that connected the ranches and the daylight was still breaking, the sunrise just starting to stop with the pinks and the oranges and start with the clear blue.

One of the three cowboys riding in the back of the bus stood and walked up to where Anderson was hiding, somewhere in the middle. He put a hand on the back of Anderson's seat, looked down at him, said, "Heard your sister skipped town."

Anderson thought, like, "Oh my god, the big kids are talking to me." He didn't say a word.

Then the cowboy went, "Too bad. John-John said that girl was a prodigy, said we could all take a ride."

Anderson's eyes went up and down like crazy. He had to say something, didn't know what, finally said, "Nicki's cool," and that was it, no more to the thought.

The cowboy said, "She went down, too. That's what John-John said. On her knees, all like…" The cowboy made a slurping sound.

Anderson's shoe flew out and kicked the cowboy in the shin.

It surprised Anderson as much as anybody, and it didn't hurt the older boy any. But that was the moment something snapped in Anderson, something glorious and large, and the first kick became a second and then another and then they became a stomping as Anderson tried with all his might to make the cowboy's knee buckle and break.

But it was Anderson who ended up face down on the bus floor. Anderson who had to watch, helpless as his backpack got tossed out the window onto the dirt shoulder. Anderson who had to come up with a story about why he showed up to his first day of sixth grade without any pens or paper.

But that first day was nothing. It was just the beginning. The worst was still to come. And it came thirty minutes to school, thirty minutes back, five days a week for two straight months.

Until finally Anderson went looking for his daddy's .357.

Anderson stood on the front steps of the six-through-senior, the gun in his backpack for the very first time, watching the hawk make patient loops over the plains, taking its sweet time choosing its prey.

Anderson was inspired. He decided not to go to class. What difference did it make? Fuck English. Fuck Algebra. He learned more from Nicki's Dead

Kennedys albums anyway.

He went around back of the school to the dock, which was the smoking area. It really wasn't supposed to be open to sixteen-and-younger, but the teachers didn't have the will to police it.

There were a couple older kids back there whispering. They looked at Anderson for a second and then paid him no attention, went back to whatever it was they were whispering about.

Anderson sat out there alone, but he felt like a part of something, like he was officially one of the bad kids, so bad they even skipped first period.

Anderson crossed his legs and stayed there on the concrete for a couple hours, hung out, watched the clouds, nodded at kids who came out to smoke, even though he'd never met any of them. Finally he got bored and went to a couple classes.

That afternoon he rode the bus home and the cowboys didn't mess with him even a little. Maybe that was because they were busy trying to convince the girls to come over after school, hang out in the basement, maybe make out a bit.

Maybe that was it.

Or maybe it was that today Anderson rode a little taller in his seat. Maybe the cowboys could sense that this would be the wrong day to fuck with the skinny sixth grader in the Mayhem shirt or pull on his long headbanger hair.

That night, Anderson waited patiently for his mom to go to bed, crept into her room. He stood there for a minute, watching her sleep, feeling the gun in his hand.

He slipped into the closet and put the .357 back in its hiding place on the top shelf. He slid back out of the room without an audible footstep, shut the door without the sound of the latch on wood. Smooth as a ninja, silent as a ghost. She never even rolled over.

Then he put on his wool cap and his coat and went out to sit on the porch and wait for his dad to come home. He shoved his hands in his pockets to keep them warm and watched the sky, imagining the hawks flying back to their nests and settling in and then the owls coming out to hunt. Anderson had never seen an owl, but he heard them all the time, and he imagined them sitting in every tree all around him, their big eyes capturing the light, tracking little movements he'd never see.

Finally there was a flash of lights on the road and the shadow of the truck bumping up the dirt drive.

Anderson's dad cut the engine and suddenly the night was so quiet Anderson could hear everything, the door squeaking open, the rubber sole on the gravel, the little grunt his dad gave as he hoisted himself out of the truck, the echo of the door swinging shut.

Anderson sat and watched, trying to notice every small thing he could, and he thought, "This is how owls live their whole lives."

Even though the two of them were thirty yards apart, Anderson's dad didn't have to raise his voice even a little for the sound of it to carry up to the boy on the porch. "What're you doing up?"

Dad couldn't hold a job and he spent more time hunting then he did keeping his house up, but he wasn't a bad guy. He never hit Anderson or Nicki after they'd passed spanking age, and he never even spoke cross around Anderson's mom. There was nothing remarkable about him, just another guy coming back from a hunt still wearing his thick camouflage jacket, his sturdy hiking boots caked over with mud.

Anderson ignored his question, walked down the steps, peered into the back of the truck. Plenty of beer cans, no deer. "Hunt go OK?" he asked.

"Went fine. Dropped my buck off at the processor."

Anderson nodded. Deer meat tasted as good as anything else. His mom could make stew out of it. And it was one more way for his dad to justify not getting a nine-to-five.

He kicked at the dirt and heard the gravel spray plink across the rim of the truck's tires. "What you shoot?"

"Twenty-two LR mostly. Three oh eight for the buck."

"Same .22 you taught me on?"

"Only one we own."

"You think you maybe could take me out

with you sometime?"

"Sure."

"Maybe we could bring your other guns, too?"

Anderson's dad looked down at him for a bit. With the truck lights cut, the man was just a big shape standing there on the drive.

Finally he reached into the bed and pulled out his backpack and his tent. He said, "Don't be in too big a hurry, Anderson. We can shoot the .22 again. Next weekend if you want." The man made a little gesture around at the trees. "No shortage of targets out there."

Anderson said, "I know."

The next day, with his dad sleeping in and his mom running around the whole house like a crazy person trying to get his lunch packed, Anderson couldn't risk going for the .357 again. He sat in his room, his arms weak and his head pounding. His backpack felt too light.

Finally, he opened his nightstand drawer and

took out the knife his dad had given him for his tenth birthday. A five-inch fixed blade, matte black, full tang, came with sixty inches of orange paracord wrapped around the handle. It was the best gift Anderson ever got, had to have cost sixty dollars. The boy slipped it into his backpack and headed downstairs.

When his mom came scurrying into the kitchen, screaming at the top of her lungs by force of habit, "Anderson, we don't want to miss the bus," she found Anderson already there, slowly eating a bowl of cereal. She looked at him for a second and said, "Oh. Morning."

Anderson nodded and kept eating.

The knife wasn't much, but it was something. The paracord around the handle made a little bulge at the bottom of his backpack, and Anderson traced it with his fingertips the whole bumpy bus ride to school.

A couple weeks later, Anderson's parents found a cat butchered in the front lawn. It had to be the neighbor's cat, even though their house was a good three hundred yards away. It was hard to tell for sure. The cat's insides were on the outside. It was missing its ears and its eyes.

Mom had found it and asked Dad to bury it somewhere. Dad went out, took one look at it, and then went inside for a bit. When he came out, he sat down in his chair on the front porch and he stayed there until Anderson got home.

The bus stop was a long mile from the house. Sometimes someone would pick Anderson up, give him a ride home. But not today. Still, he was feeling OK. He wasn't beaten up too bad. Just a, "You suck even more cock than your slut sister," and one bruise starting to blue on his shoulder. Didn't matter. He had the knife to keep him proud.

Soon as he stepped off, he could tell the weather was about to turn. Some of those big cloud walls were coming in off the Tetons, the dense and dark gray ones filled with snow. Anderson had on a fleece but it didn't do him a ton of good. He pulled his wool cap down, made sure it covered his ears, and started to walk home.

He could see his dad sitting on the porch a quarter mile away. It wasn't like the man to sit somewhere too long without a beer or a friend to talk things over with. What could be wrong? Nicki? Did something happen to Nicki?

Anderson sped up, almost to a dead sprint by the time he hit the driveway and ran past the truck up to the porch.

His dad stared him down, eye to eye for several seconds until Anderson wilted. The boy looked at his sneakers.

He felt his dad's hand on his shoulder, spinning him around to face the front yard. "You do that?" he said. And he gave Anderson a shove off the porch, sent him stumbling down the stairs into the lawn.

He took a few more steps and then he saw the cat. It was too cold for bugs, but not quite cold enough for the corpse to freeze over so it just sat there, a mess of meat in the browned-out grass.

"You do that?"

The voice was right in Anderson's ear. He hadn't heard his dad come up behind him. His eyes were fixed on the cat.

"No," he said, turning around. And then, "Maybe coyotes got it."

It was the first and only time Anderson's dad ever hit him. Anderson could tell his old man had pulled the punch a bit, and he'd learned enough getting his ass kicked every day to lean into it, shorten its power. But it was still a grown man's fist on an eleven-year-old's face. Anderson fell down, his left hand landing inches from the guts and bones.

"No fucking coyote makes cuts that clean. Think I'm an idiot?"

He reached down, slapped the cap off Anderson's head, grabbed him by both collars and lifted him up, twisting his shoulders to force his eyes at the animal.

"Think I never skinned a fucking carcass before? You tell me you did that!"

"No."

"Tell me!"

"I didn't."

Anderson closed his eyes, waiting for another punch. But nothing happened. His dad set him back down on the dried grass of their dead lawn.

"Bury it," the man said. And then he walked back into the house.

Anderson ran up the stairs, washed the dirt off his hands, threw his backpack to the floor, sat on his sister's bed and cried.

The house was real old. There was a vent went straight down from Nicki's room to the kitchen and Anderson tried to ignore the voices, but eventually he got down on his hands and knees and put one eye up to the metal slats. He could see his mom and dad sitting at the little circular kitchen table, drinking beer, staring in opposite directions, trying to make their private hells meet up somewhere in between.

"It's my fault," Anderson's dad said. He took a drink of his beer. "He's been trying to come out hunting with me for two years. Two years. Keep telling him no. Probably just wanted to see if he could do it, dropped the cat with the .22, tried to process it himself."

Anderson's mom shook her head. Her voice was trembling and her eyes were looking out the window, waiting for the snow to start piling up. "I don't know. That music he likes, have you tried to listen to it?"

Anderson's dad shook his head.

"I mean really listened to it? To the lyrics?"

The man shook his head again. He'd never taken any interest in Anderson's interests. He'd just been biding his time, waiting out the years, waiting for Anderson to get old enough they could do the things that men did together.

"It's disgusting." She paused and said, "I tried to look up some of the lyrics. All about death and dying. Having sex with dead people. Murdering women, prostitutes." She couldn't go any deeper. "They scream so you can't understand, but when you read the lyrics, it's disgusting. We shouldn't let him listen to it."

"Music doesn't make you do something like that. Something else, got to be."

"It puts ideas in his head. Makes it seem ok, like a thing people do."

They sat, drinking their beers.

After a time, Anderson heard his mom say, "He doesn't do anything anymore."

"He's a boy."

"No. I have been thinking this, thinking for a long time. He's not the same and you don't see it. You don't. Other boys are in the 4H. And he quit soccer. Other boys do things. I don't think he has friends when he's at school anymore. The new school. I think he's having a hard time with the kids, the bigger kids."

"Why do you say that?" And then in the same breath, "School is easy compared to the real world, good place to learn to stand on your own. He's my son. He knows how to stick up for himself. Damn well."

"When he's home, he just sits there, in his room or in Nicki's room. He sits in Nicki's room for hours when you're not around. Sits there. Sometimes he reads but sometimes he just stares at, at nothing. At nothing! And when you are around, he still sits, just in the kitchen or the porch, wants to be near you."

"You saying this is my fault? You're the one took four twelves instead of a normal schedule. The one not even cooking us…"

Anderson's dad trailed off. He didn't believe his own argument. He was just saying things, fighting battles he didn't believe in, trying to find some way to organize his confusion.

She sighed, too drained to even try to pretend to fight. She just looked at the snow and worried, "There's something else."

"What?"

"Couple days ago, I found something. A baggie filled with something. I found it in his room, under his bed. I think it was drugs."

Sin's insides went cold.

The baggie'd been full of meth, he knew that much. There was a guy hanging out at the dock one day, a kid who'd graduated a couple years before. The guy gave the baggie to Anderson to hold, said he'd be back for it in a day or two. But when Anderson agreed to hang onto it, then the guy told him he could use it if he wanted, wouldn't have to smoke it or anything, just mix it with some juice.

Anderson had nodded. Sure. Why not? Fuck it, right? But he'd never got around to it. He couldn't tell if he was more scared of his mom finding the baggie, or what the guy would do if he found out Anderson'd lost it. He should be back any day now.

"Drugs? You sure? Where is it?"

"I threw it away."

"You threw it away?"

"I didn't know what to do with it."

"Did you say anything to him?"

She shook her head. "He doesn't have any games or balls or anything, just that knife you gave him when you went up to the mountains back a bit."

"The knife. I forgot."

Anderson heard his dad's chair squeak as he pushed it out and then footsteps coming up the stairs.

He looked in Anderson's room first, then Nicki's. When he found the boy sitting there, he said, "Where's the knife?"

Anderson's backpack was at his feet.

"What knife?"

"Your knife. The one I gave you. Looked for it

today before you got home. Couldn't find it in your room. Where is it?"

Anderson swallowed, tried to say, "Lost it."

"Don't do this." His dad was staring him down again, little brown eyes, hard grown man eyes looking right at Anderson.

Anderson didn't even own his foot anymore. It moved by itself, pushing the backpack across the floor. Anderson's dad reached down, picked it up, pulled out the knife. He unsheathed it and looked at the blade.

Clean.

"You taking this to school?"

Anderson had no answer.

"What are you doing, taking this to school?"

The boy just looked at the floor.

His dad pushed the knife into his pocket and walked back down the stairs, sat back down with his wife at their shitty linoleum kitchen table.

Right away, Anderson stopped caring whether they thought he killed the cat or not. Didn't matter.

He started shaking. He was so scared. All he

could think of was the bus, the next morning, how he was going to survive, and finally just the one thought, "I have to get the gun back."

CHAPTER THREE: ARIZONA, 2011

"Picture yourself floating in a cloud. Your whole body is light and relaxed. Your arms are relaxed, lying gently at your side. Now our heads relax into the floor as if they were supported by the soft, warm cloud. We imagine the cloud to be purple. Everything you see is a sweet, rich purple. Sweet and rich and warm and soft all around. Take a deep breath and breathe in the purple. Breathe deeply and hold it. Let your breath linger in this liminal space, let the purple fill your lungs, then your legs, all the way down to your fingers, and finally your mind. Let the purple cloud fill your mind. And now find the blackness lingering in your body – it may be in your chest or in your head just behind your eyes – find it and gently relax, exhaling, letting go of the black and letting the purple take its place so your whole body has the sweet purple wafting inside of it."

Twelve bodies, flat on the floor of an oakwood gazebo, the curtains drawn open to let the dry desert air wash across their skin. Nine women, three guys. Five with cancer, headwraps covering bare scalps. Most of them had work done at some point, overfilled lips or tucked up eyes, the women with breasts too firm for their ages.

The thirteenth body, the teacher up front, she looked all right though. Forty, yeah, but natural at least.

Sun still wasn't quite all the way up. Doors to Denzhone's front lobby were locked. Cooks, housekeepers and dishwashers were just beginning to filter in the back.

Sin crouched, a shadow inside the shadow of a palm tree, watching the yoga class go on for a little bit. He tried to picture lying on the floor with them, breathing in the purple and exhaling black. Eventually there'd be nothing left inside that was actually him anymore. He looked at the tattoos on his forearms and his hands and the black polish on his fingernails and noticed how they camouflaged his skin. Wasn't why he'd got them done. Just a side benefit.

Sin tried to breathe in some purple and instead caught scent of something else. Eggs and waffles. His only meal in a day had been the drive thru burger he'd had last night. He rose and walked up a flagstone path around the gazebo. It led through some brush that had been culled back, and emptied out at a small building with a giant patio.

The patio was covered with sweeping blue awnings that shaded maybe thirty tables. Along the edge, servers were setting out stainless steel platters and opening them to reveal wonderful foods. Some eggs and breakfast meats, a few muffins, lots of tropical fruits, pineapples and kiwis. There was a whole other table filled with plain white yogurt surrounded by nuts and honeys and berries.

Sin watched for a second. Nobody seemed to be checking anybody's room key. He gave his shirt a tug to make sure it was covering the pistol grip, walked the last hundred feet up onto the patio, got a plate, and helped himself.

Sin chose a table along the edge of the little building and sat with his back to the wall. From there, he could see out across the patio to the desert, where the ground rose and dropped unpredictably. There were trails everywhere, winding off into the wild. Denzhone had kept the natural desert rock and dry brush thick enough that Sin couldn't see far into it, or tell very well which of the trails led to the front desk, the rooms, the pool or the tennis courts.

There was one family eating with golf cleats on, even the kids who were eight or maybe ten. Everybody else on the patio seemed old. Some healthy, with thick grey hair and tennis rackets leaning against their chairs. Others, you could tell Denzhone was a last ditch attempt to keep death from ringing their doorbell.

There was constant motion in the building behind him. It was quiet motion, but Sin could hear it and almost feel it. It was fuzzy and scattered, and it got more complex as more and more people came up on the patio to get their breakfasts.

Sometimes Sin could swear he had eyes in the back of his skull. He could feel when there was a different sort of motion in the building behind him, one more purposeful and directed at him. He turned his head a bit and saw a woman walking out. Hispanic, thick black hair pulled back in a ponytail, white polo shirt with a Denzhone logo on it.

She came up to him and asked him if he was done and could she clear his plate.

He nodded. Why not?

"My name's Maria," the woman said. "I try to meet the guests at check in. Maybe I missed you?"

"Not a guest, really," Sin said.

"Oh?" she asked. She didn't seem surprised, but she didn't seem insincere either.

Sin said, "My uncle's staying here. I had to come up to see him, no one can get hold of him a couple days. The front wasn't open."

"So you thought you'd eat?"

He nodded. It was what it was.

"The breakfast buffet is for guests," she said, but she said it halfheartedly, mostly because Sin wasn't volunteering any resistance.

He nodded again. Said, "OK, sorry about that." It was like judo.

Maria was only twenty-eight, maybe thirty. And while she tried to downplay it with her spa-issued polo and her simple ponytail, she was about the prettiest woman at Denzhone.

She walked Sin off the patio and back around the building towards the front office, asked for his ID and took it somewhere for more than an hour while Sin leaned against a stucco pillar, angled his body to stay in the shade, and squinted out into the sunshine. Finally she appeared again. Her white shirt glowed in the sun, making her almost impossible to look at.

In her hands, she held a cane.

She said, "It appears your uncle isn't here anymore. There aren't any bags in his cabana. This was the only thing we found."

Sin took the cane. It was custom-cut more

than an inch thick and weighed a ton. The handle curved to a sharp point; swung hard, it'd puncture skin, put a hole in somebody more than a couple inches wide and that was before you ripped it back out. There were sidecuts all the way from top to bottom so you could get a grip on it anywhere you needed. Years and years ago, el Viejo had taken the cane to an artist who'd embedded two little chunks of turquoise in the handle. Turn the cane just right, the point of the handle looked like the beak of a hawk and the jewels were its pitiless blue eyes.

Sin's breath got shallow. He ran numb fingers up and down the length, trying to hide trembling hands. He mumbled, "This is the only deadly weapon a citizen can legally carry on an airplane. People who need a cane like this can't get around without it."

Maria listened to him, but she didn't hear what he was trying to say. She asked, "Perhaps you could return it to him?"

He said, "Yeah," but he meant no. He took a deep, deep breath, held it in for a count of four, and then let it go. He said, "Can we look at the room, just doublecheck Harrison didn't leave anything else?"

She nodded and they walked, circling around the guest quarters on a hardened dirt walkway. It was nearly eleven and the shadows had receded into nothing. Everything that wasn't dried dead was a washed out white.

They walked in silence for a bit, but as they neared the guest entrance to Denzhone, Maria said, "Did I help? I feel like I wasn't much help."

Sin tried to put on an act for her. "It's not like Uncle Harrison to go somewhere without telling us. Do you have any idea when he might have left Denzhone?" The words felt stupid coming out of his mouth, obviously fake to the point of appearing rehearsed. He breathed through it and waited.

Maria didn't seem to notice his awkwardness. She kept her eyes on her feet, watching her step, and she said, "I'm not sure I know. Most guests set their own schedules. I remember seeing him on the dining patio a few nights ago."

They walked up off the hardened dirt onto a little sidewalk that led them to a series of buildings, each with three or four doorways. Maria stopped at one, checked the number on the keycard, and said, "Here we are."

The doorway was good, solid wood with a deadbolt and rubber tubing along the bottom to keep the AC in and the dirt out. The floor, white marble tiling in every room. Imported from a quarry in Italy, Maria said.

The art on the walls was mostly Hopi masks and Navajo blankets. One Georgia O'Keefe painting because tourists expected it. Lean the cane against the wall, it would've looked like it was art that came with the room, not belonged the person staying there.

Sin walked into the bedroom, looked around at the big king bed with the smooth white sheets. The master bathroom had an exterior shower surrounded by three high red clay walls. You could shower naked in the sun if you wanted to.

Sin walked back into the main room. It was cool, cold even, and he could hear the hum of the air conditioner. The entire back wall was constructed out of glass. On the other side, there was a marble patio and a firepit. Past that, just more brush, cacti two and three feet apart, grasses clinging onto a little hill that sloped down and then out into the desert.

Sin said, "How do I get out there?"

Maria waved her hand over a trackball set into a hardwood coffeetable. Slowly the entire glass wall rolled right, opening the whole room up to the day and the desert and the white sun.

Sin walked out on the patio. Like that he could feel the daylight on his face and his arms. Seconds later, his black t-shirt started to absorb the rays and heat up.

He walked to the edge of the patio, set his shoulder bag and the cane down, and slid into the brush.

He heard Maria say, "Where are you going?" But Sin didn't answer. He kept walking, trying not to slip on the loose rock, to keep his clothes away from the brambles and the thorns.

About fifty yards out he turned around and fished in his pocket for the photo la Calavera had given him. He held it up and squinted back at the deck. Nope, he wasn't far enough away yet.

He walked another thirty yards out and ten to

the left. He was pretty far down the slope by this point; when he squatted the patio disappeared. He stood back up.

The line of sight wasn't great, the chair blurry through the brush. The resort was quiet enough a shooter would have needed a suppressor. And nobody likes lobbing rounds up a hill. Still, the photo was taken at night and it wouldn't have been a hard shot if you had any training at all. With a scope and a stand, the degree of difficulty went down to practically nothing.

Sin slid left until he could see Maria standing on the patio. She looked about two inches tall.

He lifted one finger, aimed, bang and bang again. He imagined her spine curling in, her chest sinking backwards, her pretty body crumpling to the stones. Blood soaking through her shirt, pooling around her neck. It'd take fifteen seconds to drop your rifle, draw your sidearm, and cover the distance to the patio. One look into those saucer eyes pleading helplessly up at you, then bang.

Sin blinked away the image. He shoved his hands deep into the pockets of his jeans, stared intently at the ground, looking for shells. But there was nothing.

He tried to think of any reason anyone would have for standing out here and taking a photo of an old man sitting on a deck, other than they needed proof they'd shot him.

When he finally walked back in, Maria was standing on the patio, hands hanging down at her sides, looking concerned. A droplet of sweat rolled down her neck from behind her ear and was absorbed into the collar of her polo.

Sin looked at the stones underneath the easy chair. There was a dark patch there, a stain sliding up against the edges of the firepit. He said, "Somebody spill something?"

She shook her head. "Coyotes, probably. Dragging a kill up here."

"That happen much?"

"Not much. The housekeeping team, they said they found an animal carcass."

"Like a deer?"

"No, just one of the marmots or something."

Sin shook his head. Too much blood for a

marmot. He said, "They had to scrub the patio."

"Of course."

"Clever fuckers," he muttered.

To which Maria said, "Excuse me?"

Sin's eyes traced their way back to the wall of the condo, seeing what he expected to see – a place where the adobe had been chipped away. Someone had dug out a bullet.

He pointed at the deep divot in the wall. Maria looked and said, "Huh, how'd that happen?"

Sin shrugged. What do you say? Seven Remington Magnum maybe. Seven sixty-two NATO probably. Best just to keep your mouth shut.

Behind Maria, the sliding glass wall still hadn't been shut. "Careful," Sin said. "You leave the door open, you let the scorpions in."

He walked through into the kitchen, where he pulled two plastic bottles of water out of the fridge. He came back out and stooped down, shoved the bottles into his go-bag. Sin looped its handles around el Viejo's cane and picked the bag up and strapped it across his chest.

Maria said again, "Where are you going?"

But Sin had no good answer. He said, "Hike," and then he walked off the patio into the desert.

CHAPTER FOUR: WYOMING, 1999

This was heaven.

Freezing cold, two inches of crusted snow across a never-ending prairie, horizons miles away, gray skies everywhere, sharp winds turning his pink twelve-year-old skin red.

Anderson had stolen the .357 again. He crunched through the snow to set up a target he'd made in the basement. A piece of plywood, cut six feet tall and three feet wide, a red dot the size of a fist right in the middle.

He stepped back twenty yards, extended one hand. The gun felt heavy in it. He reached out with his other palm, tried to cup it beneath his fist. His hands were already turning red in the cold, his fingers going numb.

He extended both arms out in front of him, squeezed one eye shut, aimed, jerked the trigger and felt the gun kick a foot high.

The bang was so big but there was no echo, the soundwaves spreading out over the field in all directions off into infinity. That was ok. There was no one within a mile. His parents weren't home yet. The nearest farm might assume someone was poaching and call the sheriff, but probably not and even if they did, Anderson'd be long gone before anyone made it out here.

The boy looked around the barrel of the gun at his plywood target. He squinted.

Nothing. Not a scratch.

He took four steps closer, extended and squeezed again.

The gun bounced high again. He waited for the ringing in his ears to stop and looked at the target. Again, nothing.

Anderson took big steps forward, firing with each one. Bang, bang, bang, bang until the cylinder clicked dry. By the time he got off the last shot, he was only ten feet away.

But of six bullets, only one had hit the target at all, low, crotch level, and way to the right.

One of six.

Where were the other five bullets? Anderson's heart started to pound. Even in the cold, constant wind, his face began to burn. He looked into the distance and could see nothing except the horizon line out there.

He imagined the five bullets racing towards it, straight lines until what? They slowed, gracefully arced to the ground, buried themselves harmlessly past the snow into the soil?

No. Every bullet had hit something.

Anderson took one more long step, kicked the target over, shoved the gun in his pocket, turned, and ran the half-mile back, his boots high-stepping, breaking through the crusted snow the whole way home.

Dear Nicki, I know why you left. All the people in this town are dumb and the boys are the worst ones of all. They are all going to die. I don't know when. But I can not take what they do and what they say about you. I bet you are having fun in New York and you should never come back to this place. No matter what happens, don't come back here.

I am a bad shot. I learned that today but I can get better. That is the first thing I am going to do. Anytime they are away I am going to practice with the handgun because that is the only gun I can sneak into school unless this goes on until I am 16 and can start driving there in a truck, but I do not think I can last that long. Also on the gun, I need to find a way to start bringing it under my jacket because I can not take the backpack with me to every class and you never know when I will be able to corner them. Plus it will be good to have it so I can practice more. If dad checks the closet I am screwed and all my plans will be for nothing but I don't think he will but if he does, you still should not come back here. I will not be here when you do. Most likely I will be dead but don't be sad because I am going to not be sad, as long as I get to punish those hick assholes for everything they did to me and also to you, my sister. I love you and I miss you every day and there is now no one here I can talk to.

Thank you for all the books and your music, they are the only friends I have.

– Anderson, your brother, I love you.

Anderson wanted to send the letter so bad. But if he did, Nicki'd come back for him, he just knew it. And then he would've ruined her life, too.

So he took the letter and walked into Nicki's room and slipped it under her pillow. He stared at the bed for a while and then walked back out. He still had to clean the .357 and replace the bullets.

The meth kid was back at school. His name was Todd and he was wearing a jean jacket even though it was freezing out and sneakers even though there was an inch of snow on the flat ground.

When he saw Anderson shuffle out the door, he cocked his head up and down. "What's up, little man?" he said.

Anderson shrugged without making eye contact and tried to angle somewhere else, over to the other side of the dock. He leaned up against a dumpster and tried to look cool, but the dumpster smelled and he could feel how cold the metal was through his jacket.

The kid followed him. "Yo, little man, what's going on, man?"

Anderson hooked his thumbs in the straps of his backpack. He shrugged again and looked off over the parking lot, out past the football field.

"Hey, hey man, I wanted to ask you something."

Anderson looked up and set his jaw but it felt all fake and so he looked back down at his shoes and said, "So ask."

The older kid was taken aback. "Well, I don't really want to yell it out, here."

Anderson didn't move. Todd walked right up

in front of him, his chest level with Anderson's eyes. He leaned in and whispered, "You, uh, you try that stuff I loaned you?"

Anderson sniffed.

"Yeah, yeah, so like, so did you?"

"Yeah, I did it all."

"Oh!" Todd got kind of excited. He bit his lip, bounced a bit. "You tried it all. You dig that shit. Because it was mine but I said you could sample it, try it out and shit, so you dig it?"

"Yeah, it was fine."

"OK! OK, man! Yeah, look, here's the thing, I have some more and shit. And, like, I need to sell some because I wanted to buy a thing. So I was wondering if you'd want some more, like as much more as whatever."

Anderson still couldn't bring himself to make eye contact. He looked past Todd's shoulder, saw a few other kids there, watching. Todd was well-known at the six-through-senior. Anderson was just figuring out why.

"No," he said. "I'm good."

"You're good? No man, if you like that, I can

give you more for like, even a few bucks. Maybe you'd just want to try some or something, maybe you didn't do it right."

"I'm good."

Todd leaned in and Anderson could smell his breath, feel his hand on his shoulder. His head started to spin a bit.

"Look, little man…"

"Anderson…"

"Right, I know. I was being nice and shit. Anderson, sure, fine. Look, I appreciate you holding that stuff for me, but, like, if you can't give it back, I'm gonna need you to front that cash back my way."

"You said…"

"No, little man, no. Look, you want some more, maybe we can work something out." Todd's grip on his jacket got stronger. Anderson tried to pull away, couldn't.

"I…"

"Listen, little man, Anderson, that cost me some money so, like, you were just holding it and shit and if you did it, I…"

Anderson stepped to the side and his feet

moved but his shoulder didn't, all pinned up against the dumpster. He felt his shoes start to scramble for asphalt beneath him and find only ice. He fell on the ground, and when he did he heard the thunk of the gun in his backpack against that ground and suddenly he wasn't cold anymore.

"Oh yeah, shit Todd," he said, voice so clear and loud every kid smoking back at the dock turned to look at him. "I totally forgot, I got your shit right here."

And then Anderson's hand was in the backpack and then it was out in front of him and it wasn't shaking at all.

Todd backed up, god he moved fast. He said, "Whoa, look…"

And then he turned and slipped. He fell on all fours on the ground, crawled forward a few feet, skittered back up, took one more look at Anderson and ran, ran like crazy, ran straight over the football field and around the bleachers, ran without stopping.

Through the sights of the .357, Anderson watched Todd run. After he disappeared behind the bleachers, Anderson turned to look at the other kids.

They were running too, scurrying like gophers scurry when they see a hawk up in the sky.

What could he do?

Anderson was running, running fast, running away from the school, hand still wrapped tightly around the grip of the .357.

He ran over the football field and down the sidewalk past six blocks of tiny wooden homes with trucks in the driveway and welcome signs hanging from rusted out screen doors.

When he reached the diner folks went to along Main, he skidded to a stop, bent over, put both hands on his knees. His lungs were burning and he could feel the sweat on his neck starting to freeze. He jammed the gun into the waistband of his jeans, pulled his shirt down over it, and walked into the diner.

When Anderson came through the door, it chimed a little bell. There were a couple ranchers sitting on stools up at the counter, men in work boots, Carhartts and wool-lined canvas jackets. Both men turned to look at him and then cocked their eyebrows at Sandy, the guy who ran the diner.

Sandy shrugged. "Anderson, supposed to be in school, aren't you now?"

Anderson just looked back at him with big wild eyes, his brain still a little numb from the cold.

Sandy patted the counter, said, "Well, why don't you sit down? I'll give you a piece of pie and then you can get on back. That sound all right?"

Anderson nodded, not knowing what else to do. Sandy went back in the kitchen and when he returned he had a plate with cherry pie on it. He put it down in front of Anderson and motioned at the ranchers. "These guys, they like coffee when they have their pie. Figure you're still a bit young for coffee." And he laughed.

The two men didn't laugh though. "Everything OK over at the six-through-senior there, Anderson?" one said.

Anderson nodded without looking up. He'd seen the men around town before, they may have even gone hunting with his dad once or twice. Couldn't remember their names though. Anderson took a bite of pie, chewed on it, tried to figure out what he was supposed to do next.

He heard the little bell ring behind him. Someone entering the shop.

"Sandy, we gotta 'mergency at... Holy shit," the voice said.

Sandy took his hands off the counter and stood up tall. He was real big for a guy who served pie for a living. He said, "Now Bart, you... What's this about?"

Anderson felt his tears coming. He didn't turn around. He knew what he'd see. Bart was the sheriff's deputy. He was only about ten years older than Anderson. Went to school with Nicki and John-John.

Bart said, "Now Anderson, you, you, you just put your hands somewhere I can see them."

Anderson had a fork in one hand, a knife in the other, tears on his cheeks, snot drip-dripping down his lips. It was all over. All his plans, everything he had meant to do, everything he'd wanted to do, he'd ruined everything. "I'm sorry, Nicki," he thought.

He heard Sandy saying, "Bart, you put your weapon away, now. He's just a boy. You just take a deep breath, think about what you're doing."

But Bart had tunnel vision, his voice was trembling, "Anderson, you, I'm a deputy and you gotta do what I say, you gotta put your hands up or behind your head or something. You got to do it now. Go on. Do it."

Anderson was quivering too hard to raise his hands. His ribs started to hurt, his hands gripped the knife and the fork so hard, tiny little fists squeezing against the cold metal.

"You, you got that gun on you, Anderson? Can you hear me?"

Now the two ranchers pushed up from their stools and backed away, and suddenly there was a circle around Anderson, Sandy in front of him, Bart behind one shoulder, the ranchers behind the other. Anderson could feel the world closing in. And he said aloud, "I'm sorry, Nicki. I fucked it all up."

"Anderson?" Sandy said softly. "You got a gun on you, son?"

"Yessir," he answered. "I'm sorry."

Slowly Sandy reached out and put his hands on top of Anderson's on the counter. He closed his fingers, all big and callused from working his whole life, real tight around the boy's wrists. "Mr. Gordon, why don't you reach in and take the boy's weapon. And Bart, you just put yours away altogether. You don't want to shoot nobody neither now."

Anderson felt one rancher carefully, carefully edge in, reach around, feel for the butt of the gun, pull it out from his waistband. It felt like Anderson was losing his best friend, watching his dog die or something, like he was all alone.

The rancher took the weapon, popped the cylinder and pushed the ejector and the cartridges fell plinking down on the tiled floor. Plink. Plink. Plink.

"No," Anderson said. Snot and tears were waterfalling down his face and when he opened his mouth, he could taste them. "No, no. Please. I need them. Please, I need them back."

Bart said, "He's, he's going to have to come with me, Sandy. I'm gonna have to call this in."

Sandy said, "Bart, Anderson hurt somebody

with that gun?"

"No, he…"

"OK, then. Nobody got to go anywhere right away. I'm going to go on, give Ander and Mrs. Kenfax a call, get them down here, see what they have to say."

Anderson bolted as soon as he felt Sandy loosen his grip. He didn't think it through. He just ran, dodging around the rancher's legs and listening to Bart babble, "Sto… Sto… Stop," as he ran past him out the door into the cold street.

No one saw Anderson for two days. He was the owl, he was the bats, he was the hawk too high in the sky for the rabbits to see. It was cold but this part of the country, a lot of people didn't even lock their doors.

He was twelve but he could get by.

The school bus pulled up on the side of a road somewhere on the high plains of Wyoming.

A boy named Scott got out, wearing his cowboy boots and his meshback hat, talking a nonstop stream of cocky bullshit at a girl named Missy.

She was pretty but not popular, a late bloomer, her body only just now starting to become a woman's. This may have been the first time she'd ever been noticed by the boy who lived next door, Mr. 4H the Gridiron God.

The air brakes made a big loud sigh and the bus started to roll down the hill. Scott kept running his mouth. "Yeah, the trophies are real big like. The steer ones, that's the ones you want though. We had one go for thirty but down in Denver at the stock show, north of a hundred is the magic number. We got my trophies, you want to see them?"

It didn't look like Missy was buying it. Her arms were folding her textbooks into her winter coat and her eyes looked at the ground through big coke-bottle eyeglasses. Mumbling something about, "Mom's out, gotta get home before my l'il brother…"

"Just c'mon in for a few." Scott put a hand on the small of her back. "C'mon in and you can warm up a bit before you walk back."

"I, no, I gotta get home."

Missy stepped away and Scott jammed his hands in the pockets of his work jacket. She started walking along the side of the road. She stopped for a second and hesitated, adolescent girl needs all pulling her apart inside. She said, "Scott, could maybe I come over some other time, tomorrow even if my mom's home?"

Tomorrow? What was that? Scott was horny right now. But he smiled anyway, fake as hell. "Yeah, sounds good."

Missy said, "OK, see you tomorrow," and turned away and stepped tiny little uncertain steps down the road.

"He doesn't get a tomorrow," Anderson thought. He pulled his head back behind Scott's barn, closed his eyes and held his breath, listening, trying to see with his ears, like bats do.

Scott's boots were heavy on the gravel that lined his driveway. They got closer as he walked past the first tree, the second tree, the wood bench, and finally – now – the barn.

Anderson made no sound at all as he dashed from his hiding place, two quick steps, planted his foot on a big rock and sprang high, high above the earth, high above Scott.

The cowboy caught the motion out of the side of his eyes, turned to see what was coming for him, what bird of prey would possibly fly this low and close.

For a second, the world was so wonderful. Anderson a silhouette, a shadow against the gray Wyoming sky.

The hawk from the sun, the owl from the moon.

Scott saw the knife in Anderson's hand, its blade a shadow too, all thick and black. His eyes got so big and round and maybe he didn't have time to be scared, exactly, but he saw who'd come for him.

Perfect.

Anderson stabbed as hard as he could, aiming at the soft flesh where Scott's neck met his shoulder. He felt the tip of the knife hesitate and then cut in. But something wasn't right. There was no helpless scream, no gushing blood.

There'd been a buckle there, the buckle on a strap, and the tip of the knife had hit it and gone sideways, sawing across Scott's jacket, slicing instead of stabbing through, drawing just a bit of blood before it buried itself three inches deep into the cowboy's shoulder.

No.

Anderson's slender body came dropping down into Scott's arms and the two fell onto the gravel together, hugging each other tight.

Scott pushed frantically, arms flailing, trying to get the boy off him. The two of them scrambled up and looked at each other. Anderson knew he was screwed. Scott was five years older, six inches taller, outweighed him by, what, thirty or forty pounds or something.

But when Anderson moved, it wasn't to run. He slid down, put one hand on the gravel and kicked at the cowboy's leg, felt the knee give a bit. He kicked again and then sprang up, digging his fingernails into Scott's face.

The cowboy turned his head, closed his eyes, and used his hands. It wasn't good technique, but he was big enough to make it work. He wrapped Anderson up and heaved, throwing the boy hard at the ground.

Anderson landed on one foot and tried to stay upright, to spring right back into the fight, but now Scott was on the attack, stomping the soles of his stupid cowboy boots down hard on Anderson's shoes and throwing a big punch that connected with Anderson's empty stomach.

It was a fight just to stay on his feet now.

Scott kept punching, and when he spoke, his voice sounded different then it'd sounded the first time Anderson had heard it months ago, back when he'd tortured Anderson by calling his perfect sister a slut who loved to give blowjobs to jock assholes. Now Scott sounded like an animal, and he said, "Going to kill you, kill you, you're dead, you're dead…"

Anderson knew he meant it. But he could see there were tears and snot and fear on Scott's face too, and inside, Anderson was at peace. He'd given his life for this: to make the boy who'd insulted his big sister cry.

It was worth it.

Scott came for him. Twice more, the cowboy kicked. Anderson tried to throw up, but there was nothing in his stomach, just bile and blood and an awful retching noise.

Scott reached down, grabbed Anderson by the shoe and dragged him down the gravel driveway, his face scraping against the dirt, into the barn where his daddy kept the work truck.

Anderson felt Scott drop his foot and he lay on the ground there in front of the big tires of the pickup, trying to curl up like a baby, gasping for air.

Scott's foot stomped on Anderson's belly again and then the same foot got smaller and then rushed closer and kicked him in the back of the head. Anderson's eyes fluttered and began to roll.

Scott was going to get something. Something big, a sledgehammer or an ax. Anderson could hear the older boy panting and sniffling.

Anderson closed his useless fluttering eyes, tried to see without them, listening to the end of his life as Scott took a big breath, grunted, heaved the hammer up into the air.

And then there was a crack.

Anderson's eyes opened again, just a slit. There was an old man standing in the barn with them. He was a big man, more than 300 pounds, wearing a wool overcoat and an ancient cowboy hat. He had something in his hands, looked like a cane, and he'd caught the sledgehammer with its crook.

The old man twisted his wrist, ripped back, and the hammer fell. The cane blurred in the dark air of the barn, came around and connected with the side of Scott's arm. There was a splintering sound and Scott whined like a dog.

Scott reached back with his other arm and pulled Anderson's knife out from where it had stuck in his shoulder and there was just a little blood on it, just enough, and he made a noise, a desperate little hum.

He rushed the giant. The cane whipped around again, hit him on the head and this time there was a sickening splitting noise so loud it echoed inside the barn, like a boulder falling a couple hundred yards into the shallow water at the bottom of a quarry. Scott didn't even whimper. He just crumpled, a pile of teenager next to Anderson on the hard packed earth.

The giant tried to kneel, but for some reason it was hard for him. Anderson heard him say, "Anderson, are you still awake?"

But he wasn't.

When Anderson opened his eyes, he was in the back seat of a Cadillac, laid flat, his legs scrunched up underneath him. He could feel the car moving very fast and he could see the moon and dark clouds racing by out the window. His head hurt and he was almost too groggy to be afraid. The first thing he said was, "I know you?"

"Of course you do, Anderson. I am your mother's brother and I have met you at least three times. Not recently enough for you to remember me well, perhaps. But I remember you."

"I kind of do," Anderson said. And he did. The man was too big and too boastful and loud to forget. Anderson had clear memories of spying on him and his parents and their friends playing hearts at their linoleum kitchen table. Lying on the floor of his sister's room, peering through the heating ducts, Nicki's warm and soft teenage body lying bellydown close beside him, watching the adults play cards and drink beer. "You're my uncle. Hamilton."

"Harrison," the man corrected him.

"Right. Harrison. From, like, the FBI."

"The Bureau was a large part of my career, yes."

"That's cool," Anderson said. "Where are we going? Are we on a trip?"

"Of sorts. You are coming to live with me for awhile, my boy."

Anderson sat up, pressed back against the seat. "We're moving in with you?"

The man shook his head. "Not we, son. You. You are coming to live with me. Your parents are staying put."

"They…" Anderson was too confused to speak. Finally he said, "My mom is going to freak."

"I am afraid she already did freak, and I am the result. Your mother loves you, Anderson. And your father, he loves you too. Very much. They called me after you disappeared, and we decided it would be best if we didn't sit idly by whilst you massacred the sixth grade." The man held up an envelope, torn open. Anderson recognized it. The letter he'd slipped under his sister's pillow. "And too, I heard an awful story about a luckless cat."

"I didn't kill the fucking cat."

"Certainly not."

"Coyotes did it."

"Be that as it may, your parents asked if I might provide you with a new environment. And it appears I arrived in the nick of time, so to speak. You're not exactly a master criminal, Anderson. Nor shall you ever be, if I have anything to say about it."

"Don't call me Anderson. You know why they call me that?"

"Of course I do. You were named after your father. His name is Ander. Hence, Ander's son. They told me this on the day you were born. They were very proud of the name – and of you, as well."

"Well, I don't want any part of his name in my name."

"Hm. Very well. If you subtract the Ander, it

is simply 'Son,' then?"

The boy thought about this and said, "How 'bout 'Sin.'"

The old man nodded slowly, wisely, thoughtfully. "Certain Native American tribes chose their braves' names at about the same age you are today, my boy. Sin suits you splendidly."

Sin straightened up a little in the car and looked out the window. Past the clouds, he could see stars. They were bright and bold in the east, millions of them out there. In the west, the horizon line wavered in the distance, the last light of the day glowing over the Rocky Mountains.

"Where we going?" Sin asked.

And the old man answered, "Sin, we are headed into the desert."

CHAPTER FIVE: ARIZONA, 2011

They were sick easy to track.

They were dragging a 300-pound body.

Sin didn't wholly believe it yet, of course. El Viejo was the real deal. The idea someone'd sniped him while he sat sunning himself on a spa patio was silly. He'd pulled the trigger on so many bad guys, it seemed sort of like irony and sort of like cosmic justice, but mostly it just seemed stupid.

Still this was a real trail and it was hard to argue with. Sin picked it up just a few feet from where he figured they must have stood and killed his uncle. Two guys, both wearing boots. No gear unless they were skinny as hell, which meant a campsite or at least a staging area somewhere nearby. If Sin just kept walking, he was going to find it.

The takers' boots were good and new and the path they took through the brush showed training. Coming into Denzhone, they'd stayed on rocks and crouched low so they wouldn't catch their shirts on the thatch's thorns. That trail often disappeared for hundreds of yards at a time.

But leaving they got sloppy. They staggered, listing downhill on occasion, their bootprints heavier in the dirt. And they were definitely pulling something heavy.

It was almost four in the afternoon when the trail finally veered out of the shade of the low desert brush and up a hill littered with sharp rocks and covered by cacti. Sin took a moment to drink one of the bottles of water and stow the empty back in the go-bag. He pulled out a floppy, wide-brimmed boonie hat and put it on to keep the sun off his ears and his face. His arms were screwed. There wasn't any sunscreen in the bag, and the only cover he had was the windbreaker and a solar blanket. As much as he didn't want to get sunburned, the water loss made either an unacceptable alternative.

Sin didn't have a map, but according to his compass he'd been tracking the men pretty much due east for four hours. Dragging a body, it would've taken two men at least five or six.

They must have been pretty strong, really cocky or totally unprepared for a guy el Viejo's size, he thought. And then another thought, this time echoing in el Viejo's big booming voice, "Don't overthink, Sin. It will only confuse you. Follow the facts."

Sin slung his bag back over his shoulders and climbed the hundred yards up the hill.

As soon as he got to the top, he dropped to his belly. There were two trailers at the bottom on the other side. A few hundred yards away from them, there were a couple battered old Jeeps, one a pockmarked black, the other some ridiculous spray-on camouflage pattern. They were parked bumper to bumper longways across a packed dirt road that led off south, all the way to the horizon.

Sin pulled a tiny pair of binoculars out of the bag.

There were two guys down there. One was a white guy with a red beard and a black cap turned backwards on his head. He had a tank top on and his skin was so pale that days in the sun had brought out not a burn, but freckles that covered him like a shotgun spray. He had a hunting knife on his belt but no firearm Sin could see.

The other guy was Hispanic and he had a revolver of some sort on his hip, a cowboy hat, and a long-sleeved plaid shirt. That alone made Sin figure him for the bossman.

The men didn't talk much and when they did, Sin couldn't make out the exact words, but they were speaking English and everything they said to one another sounded like they were bored out of their skulls.

Meth, he thought at first. The front trailer is where they live and the back one is a cookhouse. El

Viejo was shot by two unwashed meth cooks because why?

No. Don't think. The desert won't forgive your assumptions.

So Sin stayed put for two hours more, dripping sweat into the dirt beneath him. He tried to be totally motionless, breathe small, slow breaths, be the hawk from the sun and the owl from the moon, waiting, watching, thinking of the men down beneath him as nothing but prey.

As dusk came on, the two men met up outside the front trailer. Their arguing got worse and finally the Hispanic guy walked five yards out into the desert and set a beer bottle on the dirt. He walked back to his partner, picking rocks up along the way. He handed half of the rocks to the white guy and motioned to him. The white guy threw a rock at the bottle, missing it by about five feet. Then the Hispanic guy threw a rock. His landed a few feet short. The white guy threw again and this time Sin heard a plink. The bottle wobbled and fell over. The white guy laughed and opened his arms in triumph. The Hispanic guy just kicked the dirt and disappeared into the front trailer. When he came out, he was holding a set of keys and he handed them to the white guy, who laughed again and then walked all the way out to the black Jeep, got in, and took off, leaving a thin trail of dust behind him. The Hispanic guy went back into the trailer.

There was no good way for Sin to get down the hill without being seen. He reached back and drew his Beretta. With his palm tight against the backstrap, he shmeared his first and middle fingers across the slide, pulling it back just enough to see the golden metal of the cartridge inside.

"One-handed brass check," he thought. "Awesome."

He flipped the safety off and reseated the weapon.

Sin stood up and started walking down the hill. His shadow stretched to his left, rippling over the rocks as he went. With his nonfiring hand, he wiped his face and his forearms until they were streaked with dirt.

He'd gotten within a few yards of the trailer when the Hispanic guy appeared in the doorway, elbow cocked, hand holding a revolver up by his ear.

Sin waved his left hand and then let it float down near the hem of his t-shirt.

"Hey, I... Sorry, I... Help. I've been out here for, since yesterday. I, I didn't... Can, can I come in? Please? I just... I got to get out of the sun," he stammered.

The man squinted at him. He didn't say anything, just pulled a breath, set his lips, and tightened his grip on the revolver. His elbow rolled forward.

Fuck.

With his left hand, Sin ripped his t-shirt up to his right armpit. His right hand drove down to his pistol and he was firing as soon as he got the barrel facing his target. In less than a second, his hands were together and his arms were locked out and he had three bullets in the bad guy.

The guy had only gotten off one shot and who knew where that went? As he fell he tried to get his revolver back on Sin, but Sin was gone.

The man gasped for air for fifteen long seconds before he died. The last thing he saw was a slender shadow edging up on his right. The last thing he felt, a shoe kicking his revolver out of his hand.

Sin took off his t-shirt and wrapped it around his left hand so he wouldn't leave fingerprints as he explored the trailer. He kept the Px4 in his right.

It was a staging area for something. Guns running down into Mexico or cocaine coming up into America. Something. Sin couldn't tell. There was a satellite phone that had to be worth two grand. Sin also found a paper log of shipments and an open box with spending cash, enough to keep the two men comfortable for a week or more.

He also found guns. A couple .38s and an ill-kept AR-15. But nothing that resembled a decent sniper rifle. Sin couldn't find any footwear in the trailer. The dead guy was wearing cowboy boots. In his mind's eye, Sin remembered the white guy wearing Timberlands. Made it unlikely this was the same team who'd dragged el Viejo six hours through the desert.

And also, no way these jackoffs took down el

Viejo. No way and Sin wanted to put his head through a window even considering it.

What Sin didn't find was a gravesite. Not near the trailer, not in the dirt a hundred yards in any direction. Whoever'd taken el Viejo must've loaded him up into a vehicle and left.

The other thing Sin didn't find was food. He thought about that for a minute. No food, close to sunset, that had to be where the white guy went. Off to get dinner.

Sin scrounged through the trailer until he found a map with directions to the nearest town. It was back northwest, not far from where he'd parked the minivan. In the trashcan, he found rib bones and sandwich wrappers and burger boxes, all from Dave's Southwest BBQ Pit & Bar.

Sin dragged the dead guy inside. Then he walked around to the second trailer. He swung open the door, Beretta up at his armpit, finger on the trigger, just in case. The trailer had been hollowed out and inside there were eight little cots packed right together. Sin backed up, closed the door with his elbow.

He walked out to the camo Jeep, climbed in the back and waited, watching the stars light up the sky, first in the east and then straight up over his head and all around in every direction, millions of white lights racing west towards a black horizon.

It was almost nine when Sin heard a motor. The black Jeep pulled up beside him, longwise, same as before, to block the dirt road the rest of the way up to the trailer. The man swung open the door and got out holding a Styrofoam box. Sin could smell beer on him. That's what'd taken so long. He'd stayed for one beer while dinner got made. Maybe more than one.

Perfect.

Sin rolled out the back of the camo Jeep and shadowed the man. He timed each footfall to land with the man's heavy half-drunk steps and smiled. He was able to get within five feet before the man sensed something was wrong and looked over his right shoulder. Sin leaned left and man turned, turned, turned until it was too late. Sin had the pistol in his left kidney and a knife at his throat. The man screamed, stumbled over a rock and fell on his back. Sin followed him down, straddling his chest and sticking his knife an inch deep in the man's nose.

"Hi," he whispered.

The man shouted, "Jaun!"

But the only answer was Sin, his voice quiet as the wings of an owl. "You shouldn't speak the names of the dead."

Sin sat on the man's chest for a second, right hand on his Px4, which he kept back against his body, close to his right armpit where it'd be hard for the man to snatch it from him. With the other hand, he lovingly twisted the knife. The man screamed and when he did Sin said, "Next sound you make, I'm going to push this knife behind your eye. Thick blade. Not long enough to hit your brain. I'll ask the same questions. You'll answer them blind. Two days ago, there was a tactical team here."

The man nodded and when he did, some snot and drool shook free and started oozing down his right cheek.

"What were they doing here?"

"I don't know."

"Where'd they come from?"

The man tried to shake his head but the knife bit into his nose. Blood began a little trickle down the left side of his face. He whimpered. "Australia or New Zealand. God, I don't know."

"What were they doing here?"

"I said I didn't know."

"How long?"

That one, he knew the answer to and he couldn't wait to say. "A night. One. They left their car and their gear here for a day and a half while they went hiking. Next day, they were gone."

"What kind of gear?"

"What?"

"What kind of gear? Hiking gear?"

"Like, military. They didn't say shit. They just dropped their stuff and left."

"When they came back, they have someone with them?"

"I said! I didn't see them!"

Sin's eyes flashed around. The night was still quiet, no one coming along the ridge or down the hill that led back the direction of Denzhone. The moon was so bright and the man's face was blue in it and his blood black.

"What is this place?"

The man shook his head no.

Sin put the knife in. Not all the way, like he said, but enough that it sliced the man's nose open. The stream of blood became a sheet that flowed up his cheek into his eye. He wiggled desperately and Sin pulled the knife back so the man could lift his left hand to the side of his face and feel the liquid.

He put the knife on the man's left eyelid and said, "It's a staging area, right?"

The white guy was too confused to say anything anymore. He wiped at his eye, lifted his head, trying to keep the blood from filling his socket. Sin had to move the knife to keep the guy from impaling his own eye on it. For a second, Sin was transfixed by the way the blood reflected a glossy black as it pooled, how it overflowed from the socket and dripped onto the sand. Sin shook the image out of his head and said, "What are you running?"

"He's going to kill me," the man whimpered.

Sin looked at him, trying to keep from laughing. Finally he said, "Yeah. Me too."

He pulled back the knife and stuck it an inch into the man's neck, away from the windpipe or the jugular. The freckled man screamed again. Sin had to remind himself to be patient, wait for him to calm down. Finally the man said, "El Diablo Rojo de la Santa Cielo. He runs them through here."

"The mercs, they worked for this Diablo?"

The man shook his head. "Our handler just called, said we were going to have guests and we needed to pick a rendezvous point in town and lead them in."

"What does he run, Diablo?"

The man shook his head, started trying to bargain. "No, no," he said.

"Drugs?"

The man nodded eagerly. "Yeah, yeah, cocaine and stuff."

Sin looked at him, puzzled. Finally he said, "It's girls, isn't it? But you let the tac team come through here anyway."

"Jesus, you know whose place this is? El

Diablo Rojo de la Santa Cielo."

"Stupidest fucking nickn…"

Sin stopped. Oh the irony.

"He made me watch, he made me watch him do it to someone, some farmer, he made me watch…"

Sin pulled the knife back to his chest and leapt into the air. He fired twice before his feet hit the ground and the bangs of the twin gunshots slid over the desert like the wind itself and hit the eastern mesa and came bouncing back to Sin and those echoes, they sounded like applause.

It was almost ten at night when Sin steered the black Jeep into the parking lot of Dave's Southwest BBQ Pit & Bar, also known as the only restaurant in town. He looked around to make sure no one was watching before he parked.

He'd kept a piece of cloth over the steering wheel as he drove, but he wiped it down anyway before he slid out of the Jeep. He tossed the cloth in a dumpster out behind the restaurant.

Sin walked in the back door and headed straight for the restroom.

His hands were trembling.

He asked them to stop. They ignored him.

He looked at himself in the mirror.

Hell. That's what he looked like. Hell.

He scrubbed up best he could. With a little hot water, the sweat came off his face and the blood washed off his hands, but he couldn't get the dirt out of his hair. He tried hard, but his fingers got stuck halfway through, meeting up with clumps of mud.

He drew the Px4 and dropped the clip, thinking maybe operating his favorite weapon would settle him down. It didn't. His hands just kept shaking as he counted nine cartridges left in the clip, plus the one in the cylinder. He holstered the gun and walked out into the restaurant.

As the only place to eat within fifty miles, Dave's didn't need to pretend to be anything special. The smell from the kitchen was just great, but that may have been because Sin hadn't eaten since he'd swiped a seven a.m. breakfast off the patio at Denzhone.

Sin walked up, pulled out a stool and sat down. A waitress came up on him and said, "What'll you have?"

Sin reached back in his memory banks. He couldn't remember what people from Australia sounded like, exactly. So he just winked and mumbled, "Bud Light and a burger, mate."

The waitress looked at him for a second, trying to judge his age. Her eyes floated down to the tattoos on his forearms and his hands. She nodded to herself and disappeared back into the kitchen without another word.

Sin looked around the restaurant. It was reasonably packed with a mix of elderly couples on road trips and townies stopping by for a bite on their way home from work. Bud Light may have been the only beer on tap, because every pint in the place was filled with a similar see-thru amber.

The waitress came back with his beer and said, "You all right, sweetie?"

He tried to think of something Australian people would say, but the only thing he could come up with was "crickey," and he was pretty sure that was just in the movies. So he just nodded. He removed one trembling hand from his pocket and wrapped it around the beer. It shook when he raised it to his lips.

The waitress was a big woman, almost fifty, long tight curls pulled back over her skull. She cocked her head. "Sure about that?"

Sin nodded again and he heard a familiar voice in his head telling him to work with what he had. Faking some sort of accent, he said, "I got separated from my camping mates out there. Had to walk out the desert myself. Lucky I found the road back."

"You been here before?"

"I didn't come in, was sleeping back of our truck. My mates did. Two lads. You see 'em?"

"Older then you, beards on both of them?"

"Sounds right."

"I saw them come through when you set out two, three days ago. They met up with some friends here."

Holy shit, it'd worked. Sin said, "Ah! That's them all right," but inside he was stunned. He thought, "El Viejo will be so proud," and then, "El Viejo would be so proud."

"If I were you, go back to the motel. Maybe they'll check in back there."

Sin ticked his head in no particular direction. "That one?"

"Oh sweetie," the woman said, "town ain't got but one motel. Now lemme go see if your burger's up."

Sin nodded and stared down into his Bud Light and saw the wide, scared eyes of the white slave trader staring back.

Sin wasn't a virgin killer. He'd shot two mobsters in a firefight last summer, very bad men and he never felt nauseous about it or had nightmares or anything. And he'd killed one other guy a year before that, a cheating spouse he'd been surveilling with el Viejo. The man'd seen them snapping photos, started screaming, and then charged them with a cleaver and it was eerie to Sin how automatic his reactions were, how quickly he'd drawn his weapon and dropped the man with two shots that, when the cops got there, he'd learned were only a half-inch apart in the man's heart. Yeah, there'd been all the drilling with el Viejo, hours at the range, days in the desert. But there was something else, too. Something that allowed Sin to pull the trigger when almost anybody else would have hesitated and got a cleaver in the face as a reward. The police had taken all Sin's weapons and held them for two months before the court ruled the shooting was self-defense. They were two of the worst months of Sin's life.

But tonight had been different. As soon as Sin'd dropped the bossman, he knew he'd have to take out the guy with the freckles. He'd planned it. And enjoyed it.

Sin polished off his beer in one long gulp. El Viejo had to be alive. He just had to be. Or else who was going to keep Sin from killing everyone he saw?

Sin felt a tap on his shoulder. He turned around and saw Maria.

She was still wearing her Denzhone-issued slacks and white polo, but the buttons had been undone and they revealed more of her smooth brown neck, her delicate collarbone, the beginnings of her cleavage, pushing up against the shirt. She'd let her hair out of the ponytail and put on some lipstick. Sin looked over her shoulder and saw a half-dozen other young people also in white polos.

Maria had a little smile on her lips. "Thirsty?" she said.

"Mm, yeah. I guess."

"Have a nice hike?"

Sin laughed a laugh that was mean and dry. "Yeah. Very."

Maria motioned down at the bag at Sin's feet. It still had el Viejo's cane lashed to the top. "You find your uncle?"

"Maybe." Sin looked back at the group of people behind Maria. They'd clustered around a pool table and the waitress with the curly hair was bringing out pitchers of beers. "Come here a lot?" he asked.

She nodded. "Where else we going to go? Some of us live in town. The college kids sometimes camp all summer, wash up at Denzhone when no one's looking."

"What about you?"

Maria pulled out the stool next to Sin, sat down and looked over at him with those big, brown eyes. She raised her eyebrows like she was sharing a secret. "I got a little place in town."

Maria's eyes were like Nicki's, big sweet saucers that could look knowing and teasing one second, soft and submissive the next. Sin swallowed hard, looked back at his glass and cursed when he saw it was empty.

Maria smiled again. She raised her voice and said, "Cindy, can me and my friend here get another round?"

The waitress looked over and raised her tray to show she'd heard.

Maria said, "We come here almost every night, not all of us, but some of us at least." She looked back at her crew. Most of them were pounding away, two or three cups into their pitchers already. "Some of them, I'm their boss. I guess I'm a bad influence. But you gotta do someone for fun around here." She batted her lashes at Sin, just to make sure he'd heard her right.

Jesus, her eyes looked like Nicki's.

Sin's heart started to go bang. He looked down at the bar and found Cindy'd managed to slide a refill in front of him without him even noticing. He picked it up. Drank.

An hour and two beers later. A round of shots. A game of pool that seemed to include most of the people at Dave's Southwest BBQ Pit & Bar. Another round of shots. A slow kiss back by the restroom. Maria whispering, "I gotta go. You want to come make sure I get home safe?"

And Sin said yes, but he was hyperventilating almost as they walked out the parking lot. The black Jeep was still there, and no one was ever coming for it. Sin tried to ignore it. He let Maria lead him to her car, a little sport wagon with a bike rack on top.

They kissed again, much harder than inside. Sin felt both her hands on his shoulders and then her fingernails, tracing their way down his chest. He took a step back.

"I don't think I can do this," he said.

"You got a girlfriend?"

"I don't know," Sin said, thinking about Sindy. "Maybe."

"Maybe?" Maria let her hands drift further until her palms were flat on Sin's belly, fingers facing down, nails toying with the buckle on Sin's belt. She bit her lip and said, "Maybe doesn't count, right?"

Sin closed his eyes, felt the pressure on the other side of his belt, the Px4 pushing up against the small of his back, his body trapped in between its heavy metal slide and the light touch of Maria's fingertips. What happened when she saw his gun?

She tugged a little bit on his buckle, pulling him towards her. "Come on," she teased. "Come home with me."

"I'm sorry," Sin said. "I can't. There's something I have to do."

"Tonight?"

"Yeah," Sin said and he wasn't lying.

One in the morning. A roadside motel. A lot full of trailers parked across two spots and semis stretched over five.

The road empty, just the headlights of the occasional trucker speeding by, taking made-in-Mexico goods up north.

Sin stopped between two semis. He zipped up the windbreaker to cover up any identifying tattoos and wrapped a bandana around his face. Then he slid the go-bag behind the wheel of one of the semis.

He climbed the chainlink fence around the back of the hotel and jumped down next to the rear exit. The door was latched, but opened with just a little jostle.

Sin crept down the hallway to the back door of the attendant's office. There was only one guy on duty, an old man with a stooped back, long white hair in a ponytail out behind him. Sin froze and stayed in position, barely breathing, for almost two minutes until he was reasonably sure the man didn't have a shotgun too close by.

Sin crawled up behind him so slowly, like a spider edging its way across the floor. When he was six feet away he said, "Don't turn around. I'm not going to hurt you."

The man almost gave himself whiplash, turning and then trying not to turn. He raised his hands by instinct, but his voice only shook a little. "Money drawer's to the right."

Sin said nothing.

"Just take it." The man repeated, "Please, just take it and go."

"I don't want the money."

"Oh, oh Jesus," the man said.

"I'm not gonna hurt you. Information about a guest."

"What do you want me to say?"

"A couple nights ago, you work here?"

"Every night. I'm always here."

"Two guys, beards, Australian. You remember them?"

The man nodded.

"You got names?"

The computer was on the desk. It had to be fifteen years old. Sin watched the man wake it up, look up an old reservation, and nod at the screen. "That's them."

"O'Reilly and Carter? They show IDs?"

"Yes."

"Passports?"

"Drivers licenses."

Fuck. Passports were more likely to be legit. The licenses were almost certainly fake. "American?"

The old man shook his head. "No. Mexican."

"Australians with Mexican drivers licenses? You sure?"

The man nodded.

"You see what kind of car they drove?"

The old man shook his head no, said, "I never saw." And then he waited. And waited. And waited. Finally he said, his lip trembling and his voice cracking, "Please, you can have all the money we have."

There was no reply.

The attendant turned around and the shadow was gone.

Sin walked all the way back to Denzhone. It was dawn when he used the spare set of keys to start el Viejo's Cadillac and wheel it out of the parking lot.

He didn't want anybody calling the police or searching after the Cadillac's owner. Not 'til he was done.

He parked the Cadillac next to the minivan, got out, locked it, and then crawled inside the van to get some shuteye. Before he drifted off, he swapped his Beretta for el Viejo's 1911. Someone was going to die and they were going to die with bullets from the old man's gun.

Sin closed his eyes.

Falling asleep in an exposed location. Again.

El Viejo would've killed him.

The next morning, Sin started up the minivan with his little rolling armory in it and drove thirty miles towards Tucson before hitting a coffeeshop. He went in and got himself a cup of coffee and then walked back out to the minivan, climbed in, and called la Calavera.

"What's the status, kiddo?"

"Doesn't look good."

"No?"

"Seems like el Viejo got into it with two guys, might be a tactical team. Couple people said from Australia or New Zealand, England maybe."

"They rogue?" the old lady asked.

"Negative. They had connections up here. Staged at a site I think was maintained by a cartel."

"Was?"

"Was."

"I see."

"Better if you don't."

Sin could feel la Calavera smile.

"Anyway," he continued, "that seem right?"

"What?"

"Australian tactical teams hanging out with Mexican cartels in Arizona."

"It does to me," she said. With half a lung and an oxygen tube up her nose, it took la Calavera a long time to explain. Sin put his cell phone on speaker and sat crosslegged on the floor of the minivan, sipping coffee, listening.

The Australians deployed almost a quarter of their special forces to the Middle East during the second Iraq War. There, American helicopters deployed the SAS Squadron and provided logistical support while the Australians captured the Al Asad Airbase. Most of the Aussies were out of Iraq by 2009, except some members of the Fourth Royal Australian Regiment – 4 RAR Commando.

After the war, lots of tip-of-the-spear guys found work with private defense contractors running VMTC's in Mexico. They were mercenaries, imported to stabilize, educate and run live-fire exercises for a Mexican police force that'd been decimated by corruption and the defection of whole units that'd started their own damn cartels.

The Australian teams had good relationships with the Americans and real theater-of-war experience in urban and desert environments. It made plenty of sense that at least a few of them would land mercenary jobs in Mexico. But once they were there, they found a world in which loyalty was nonexistent, cash was everywhere, and the person with the biggest guns ruled. It was easy to imagine mercenaries demanding favors from the same cartels they were training rookie Mexican cops to hunt.

By the time la Calavera ended her story, Sin

had finished his coffee and was staring down at his phone on the floor of the minivan. He took it off speaker and held it back up to his ear. "Yeah, so what do I do?" he said.

"Try Yuma. If they're heading back across the border, they'll stop there."

"Copy that," Sin said and tapped off his phone.

CHAPTER SIX: YUMA, 2006

When they first got to the Yuma Proving Grounds there'd been lots of quiet conversations, lots of Sin watching el Viejo from a distance. Seeing him shaking hands, clapping backs, saying thank yous. But now, all the conversations were over and the quiet was gone.

Time to rock and roll.

Sin, sixteen years old, wearing his Cynic t-shirt and black jeans, the same stuff he wore to school pretty much every day. But today was different. Today he was owner of a report card with passing grades in every subject for the first time ever. And this was his reward. El Viejo'd called in some favors and gotten him a front row seat to a tactical training session at the Yuma Proving Grounds.

It was the largest military training installation on the planet, thirteen hundred square miles of sandy desert washes and craggy mountain ridges. No commercial flyovers. No elderly homeowners calling their congressperson to complain about how the roar of the air sorties disturbed their pet poodles. Thirteen thousand missile, mortar and artillery rounds fired every single day.

Every single day.

This wasn't no Behind The Big Guns Tour. They'd done that last year. This was the real thing. Sin and el Viejo were bouncing madcap across the desert in an assault vehicle at fifty-five klicks. On the benches next to them, a sixteen-man squad. In the soldiers' hands, H&K MP5's loaded with live rounds.

The sergeant serving as tactical command

said everything very loudly, barking at Sin and el Viejo, shouting above the roar of the engine. "Today we are conducting a training exercise with members of the Canadian Royal Air Force. The structure to your lefthand side was built to resemble a village in Afghanistan, which is a typical environment into which these men might be deployed. A member of the 2nd Commandos will be playing the part of a high-value Al-Qaeda target. The mission is to extract this target safely to a bird located north of the structure. When this vehicle stops, this team will deploy and you will remain seated. I repeat, you will remain seated. There are glasses underneath your seats. I hope you men enjoy your afternoon."

The sergeant stood up taller and called out orders to the sixteen soldiers. "Gentlemen, make weapons ready. We are go in sixty." And seconds later the vehicle skidded to a stop, tires gripping into the dirt. The men poured out of the truck, boots landing on hardpack, the first man with his MP5 to his cheek, everyone behind him muzzles pointed down, moving and then fanning out and lifting their sights as they approached the adobe structure.

Sin watched from inside the assault vehicle, panting shallow breaths, as one man stepped in with the handram, counted two, swung and splintered the wooden door.

When he heard the first claps of a firefight, Sin grabbed the binoculars and he couldn't help it, he stood up, took a step forward, and leaned out of the vehicle to get a better view. El Viejo put a hand on his shoulder, pulled him back inside.

"What do you think, son?"

Sin just looked at him wild-eyed for several seconds. Then he said, "This is awesome."

El Viejo smiled. He had to yell to be heard above the sounds of the drill and the roar of the motor. His voice echoed around the inside of the assault vehicle. "The real weapon isn't the guns. It's the team."

"You see those MP5's?"

"You have to stop seeing weapons as a fetish, Sin. You must learn to see them as soldiers see them. As tools that help the team accomplish an objective."

Sin leaned forward. Pushed his face to the very edge of the open door of the assault vehicle. Felt the light of day hit him like god would hit him if they ever met. Sin was shaking, dying to jump out of the vehicle and get into the fight.

"Don't trust your feelings, son," el Viejo yelled. "These men aren't killers; they are soldiers. They do not live looking for a fight; they live in Condition Yellow. Aware and alert, at one with their environment."

Sin ignored that bullshit entirely.

El Viejo paused, trying to get his thoughts together. Finally he said, "Have you thought about it?"

"What?"

"Joining the military when you graduate from your high school."

Sin dropped the binoculars and turned around. "What do you mean?"

"You'd go far, Sin, if you chose that path. Special forces, if you like."

"But why can't I stay with you?"

El Viejo didn't want to yell, but it was the only way he could make himself heard. "I have been thinking, Sin. Thinking a lot about you. My body has not been kind to me as of late. Someday I must retire. Soon, likely. And I was thinking, what will become of you?"

"You want me to leave?"

"No," el Viejo said, starting to realize he'd made a terrible error. He wanted to pull Sin aside, to speak to him quietly, but that wasn't going to happen here. There were helicopter blades whoomp whoomp whoomping two hundred yards away. "No. I only mean that you will need to learn a trade, something you can do to support yourself. And the military is a place where you'd find structure. And where you could put to use everything I have taught you."

And suddenly, the tactical commander yelled, "Ceasefire!" The helicopter blades started to rise, to quiet. The soldiers left on the ground were moving back to the vehicle, getting closer.

"But I'm going to work with you," Sin said. He took a step back inside the van and stood facing el Viejo, his body silhouetted against the bright sunlight streaming in from the door. The only sound outside now boots on sand. "You said I could."

"My body isn't willing to carry me across this land chasing evil men much longer. Someday – someday soon – you will need to find another path."

Sin shook his head violently. "No, I won't go. Please don't make me go."

"Sin, relax, my boy. It was just an idea. You have two more years before you'd even be able to enlist. Please, just relax."

But Sin couldn't relax. He squeezed his eyes shut and he clenched his fists so hard because they felt empty and he wished he had something in them, anything.

"I won't go. I'll kill myself. I'll kill myself if you make me go."

The soldiers had stopped in their tracks and now they were standing just outside the vehicle, trying to ignore the scene, looking at the sergeant for some sort of guidance, but even he was just staring at Sin. The boy was standing and trembling in the doorway to the assault vehicle.

El Viejo took a step back and sat down on one of the benches, trying to give Sin more room. "Sin, please take it easy. It was just an idea."

"I hate it. I hate that idea. It's a stupid idea. I hate it," Sin said and he collapsed to the floor, squirmed back up against the side of the assault vehicle.

El Viejo sat, numb and without a weapon for the very first time in a long life spent finding things and fighting things.

He watched as Sin cowered against the frame of the vehicle, pulled his scrawny knees up to his chest, wiped back a tear and whimpered, "Please don't make me go, el Viejo. I want to stay here with you."

El Viejo climbed off the bench and eased his aching body down on the floor. He wrapped an arm around Sin's shoulders. "You don't have to go, son. I'm sorry." The old man looked out the door at the soldiers in their helmets looking in. He cast his eyes up at the ceiling of the vehicle and said, "I just don't know what to do with you once I'm gone."

CHAPTER SEVEN: YUMA, 2011

Sin drove south an hour or two and then wheeled the minivan west. Before long, the low desert became just plain old desert. The shoulder-high brush gave way to knee-high creosote; the knee-high creosote gave way to sand. The occasional oak became the lonely saguaro. The mesas to the north dropped beneath the horizon and Sin was left with a three-hour drive on a flat patch of baked earth.

It'd been years since he'd been to the Yuma Proving Ground. The entrance was way around on the western edge of the Sonoran Desert, towards where it climbed up into the Mojave. There was a low brick wall and a sign that popped up out of nowhere with the words "Yuma Proving Ground – United States Army – Cornerstone of Test & Evaluation."

Sin started there and worked his way north towards Yuma, stopping at the Holiday Inn, the Embassy Suites, whatever hotels and motels he found along the side of the road.

El Viejo'd taught him, use what you got. Some guys were smart and had detective skills. Some guys were friendly and had people skills. But all Sin had was stealth and that didn't do him any good out here. The day was too bright and he didn't have the time to stake out each and every place his quarries could be staying before sneaking back across the border into Mexico, where they'd almost certainly be able to disappear for a very long time. At that first hotel between the Proving Grounds and Yuma, Sin sat in the minivan for almost fifteen minutes, trying to plot out a way to get the information he needed without actually having to talk to anybody.

Wasted time.

In the end he walked in, dangled his car keys in his hand, and asked the lady at the front desk, "Hey, you got two guys here from Australia? They left their keys at the info center."

He was shocked beyond belief when the lady answered sweetly and candidly. She said, "Sorry, hon. Not here."

OK, then.

The next hotel had been only slightly more complex. The guy there said he only worked the day shift and couldn't be expected to know everybody in the hotel. Sin said, "Come on man, they got me runnin' all over town trying to find these two. Australian I think, maybe English or something. They both got beards." The guy sighed, looked at his computer and said, "Nobody's checked in with a Pacific Theater passport of any kind."

"Nah, they were using Mexican driving licenses. Names were O'Reilly and Carter, I think that's what they told me on base."

"Oh, hm," the guy said, he scrolled back through his computer screen. "Nope, not that either.

Sorry kiddo."

"It's OK." Sin nodded and walked back out of the hotel.

He put on the show again. And again. And again. Three chain hotels. Four motels no one without a weapon should even consider staying at.

Nothing at any of them. Sin was out of options.

Sin walked out a Quality Inn. The eastern sky'd turned smooth shadings of purple and the western was a wash of yellow, but here on earth the light was flat and indistinct, no shadows cast out of the dim gray.

He spied a diner across about five hundred yards of connected parking lots. He was hungry as hell. He had EDC gear on him – the 1911, a pocketknife, a pocket flashlight, keys, wallet, phone, that's all. But he felt fine about leaving his stuff in the minivan for a bit so he could get some food, sit down a minute, plan his next move.

Walking across the parking lot, he started to think, "They're gone. Ghosts over the border, on to the next job." He tried to beat back the hopeless feeling in his stomach, say it was just hunger and he'd feel fine once he had some food in him. He started to make plans for a border crossing. Stash his stuff at his apartment, try to get a weapon once he was in Mexico. He had some friends over there, people who could set him up and maybe even put him on the right path. He could start in trying to find Policia Federal VMTC's. Or start making noise about la or el Diablo Rojo de la Santa Something. See where that got him, as long as it didn't get him dead.

He barely saw the guy holding the door open for him had a beard, a shirt with a long tail, the butt of a pistol printing against his flannel. But he did and when Sin walked past the guy said, "See the booth at the end? Move there now. Hands out your pockets."

Sin could have kicked himself. Stupid flat light at dusk, it makes everything tricky. No shadows, no depth perception. He blinked as he walked into the diner and when his eyes adjusted saw a guy sitting in the booth in back, also with a beard.

The guy behind him said, "Go."

And Sin went.

He slid into the booth and the first guy sat next to him and slid a fixed blade from his flannel sleeve, buried the tip of it in the skin just on top of Sin's femoral artery.

Sin looked over at him. The man had streaks of gray in longish hair and wrinkles around his eyes and across his neck.

The guy across the table was a bit younger, maybe forty. He had a crewcut. He had one hand on top of the table, wrinkled and freckled and stained brown from four decades in the sunshine, and he was wearing a black and white paracord bracelet on his wrist along with a tac watch. The other hand, his right hand, was hidden under the table and when the man saw Sin looking for it, he tapped. Sin heard metal on plywood. Some sort of handgun aimed at his belly.

Sin looked back and forth from the knife in his thigh to the gun aimed at his gut and then he muttered, "Kind of overkill."

The guy sitting next to Sin talked. The other guy's eyes started flashing left and right, his head on a swivel looking for anybody who might be looking back.

"You're not who we expected, mate," he said. "Where'd you serve?"

"I'm not in the army."

"Civilian?"

Sin shrugged.

"You can't get good help these days," the Aussie said and it sounded like a joke, but his partner didn't laugh.

Instead he said, "Incoming."

The guy with the longer hair pulled the knife under the napkin in his lap. When Sin looked up, there was a waiter standing there, a skinny old man, bald, a faded anchor tattoo on his forearm. He flipped pages on his pad and said without looking at them, "What'll it be?"

Sin said, "I think I'm going to need a beer."

The waiter replied, "ID."

While Sin pulled out his license, the waiter turned to the Aussies and said nothing, just looked at them. The one with the longer hair said, "Nothing for me now."

And the waiter, still not looking up, said,

"You have to order food to sit."

The man sighed, just a little sigh. He looked at the menu leaning against the window and said, "This top thing, the special."

"Chicken and waffles, coming up."

The man with the crewcut looked at his partner, a little smile on his lips. "Waffles?"

"Oh fuck off," the first guy spat. And then to the waiter he said, "They'll 'ave the waffles too, all right?"

"Three specials. What're you men drinking?"

They ordered water and that was all.

As the waiter turned around, the guy with the long hair tapped Sin's thigh with the knife again, just to remind him it was there, and he said, "You bring our money?"

Sin paused way too long. "Yeah, I think so," he said. He looked at the guy's faces, trying to read if they'd heard the pause, knew he was lying and when they glanced at each other Sin thought, oh my god I am going to die tonight.

But the man with the long hair spoke and he said, "You're not what we were expecting."

Sin said, "Look, I didn't sign up for this."

"What do you mean, mate?"

"I mean I didn't sign up for this."

"You're a courier, not a bag man."

"I just said I'd give you a package. I don't know what's in it."

"If you say so," the man said but then he leaned over, whispered in Sin's ear, "But don't tell me you don't have a pistol in your waistband, mate."

"Yeah," Sin said, his eyes going back and forth between the man with the knife and the man with the gun. "It's my uncle's."

The guy across the table had taken a drink of water and he almost spit it out all over the table. He said nothing though. Just ran the back of his hand across his mouth, wiping it dry.

The guy with the knife looked into Sin's eyes real hard. "Your uncle's?"

"My... I thought maybe I should have one, you know? Guy just said he'd give me a whole grand to deliver a package. I don't know what I'm getting into, right? But in my car, I have it."

"No," the man shook his head. "What guy?"

"What guy? Some guy, said he was with a Diablo," Sin said.

The two men exchanged glances. One rolled his eyes, the other nodded. The man withdrew his knife, slipped it silently into a sheath he had stowed somewhere up his forearm. He leaned back and said, "You're all right, mate. Listen, best not let that fat fucker hear you not using his complete name."

Sin rolled his eyes just like the Aussie had and the two men laughed and Sin could feel them relax. The guy with the crewcut shifted his arm back a bit and laid the pistol in his lap.

"Yeah, you're all right, mate," the one next to Sin repeated. "You just don't know who you're working for. Let's let you finish your beer and get all done with this, we'll be on our way, yeah?"

Sin said, "Can we do it? Now? I want to go."

"Whoa, now. My waffles aren't even here."

The merc laughed, laughed right at him. And Sin thought, you're not in Condition Yellow now are you, bitch? But what he said was, "You can... Come on, I just want to get going. I didn't sign up for all this."

The guy with the knife said to his partner, "I'll go. You stay. Eyes..." He ticked his head out the window and the guy with the crewcut nodded.

Slowly the man got up from the booth and Sin slid out next to him.

The parking lot wasn't quite empty and it was not dark but darkening. One or two truckers milling about, keeping their eyes on their own business as Sin and the Aussie walked through rows of semis and SUVs, the occasional Subaru with a kayak or bikes on top.

Sin was in front and he spoke over his shoulder, said, "You know, you should look at this gun."

"I should?" the man said.

"Because my uncle, he's dead and I don't know what to do with it and he said once, maybe it might be worth something."

As they walked between two semis, Sin reached back and drew the weapon backwards and upside down, like he was just gripping it, his little finger near the trigger, the barrel parallel to the ground beneath it. A 1911, cocked and locked, but upside down, no way the man could see anything but a dumbass kid holding a pistol all wrong. Sin stopped, turned, said, "You see this gun?"

The man ripped his flannel up, had his USP up eye-high and his sights on Sin within half a second. He stepped to the side, trying to get to where Sin's barrel wasn't pointing at him, but the semis were parked too close together and in that canyon he couldn't get far. He kept both hands on his USP and took a step back, instinctively trying to stay an arm's length from Sin. "I do. Now put it down."

"Whoa, hey," Sin said. "No, I was hoping you could help me out? My uncle left me this gun, and I was sort of wondering if someone like you might know what it's worth?"

"You put that back in your trousers. We can look at it later."

"I just want to get going. I have to... Can you... Just look at it."

Sin held the weapon out, barrel first, keeping his windbreaker sleeve down. The barrel was tilted down at an odd angle, at the man's gut.

The Australian guy with the long hair talked

as he squinted at the gun in the dark parking lot. He said, "Be careful where you aim that weapon, boy. That's a man's gun."

"It sure was," Sin said.

Sin swept his arm up and pushed the sights of the USP off target and then he shot O'Reilly or Carter or whatever he said his name was. Shot him from just six inches away, got to see what a .45 does to a man's abdomen when it punches him from that close. Big slow caliber, tears a hole the size of candlestick, ripples through his guts, the path of the bullet spreading until it's big as a tennis ball. All the water in O'Reilly's body rushed to the surface. His face ballooned blue.

Sin heard the USP go off, heard glass breaking and metal thunking by his head. He flipped the 1911 around to his right hand and pulled the trigger again. Nice snappy single action. It hit the mercenary in the neck as he curled over and stumbled backwards. Lodged somewhere near his spine. It threw him rigid again, back into the semi cab behind him, cracking the passenger side window, denting the door, setting off an alarm.

Sin looked up to see the other Aussie coming out the door of the diner. People all around were looking around, trying to figure out what had happened. Military town, nobody was mistaking this for engine backfires or anything like that. Who knew how many concealed weapons within two hundred yards. Maybe a dozen, lots of them in the hands of trained US military personnel.

Sin dropped to his belly on the dark ground, rolled under the semi, and crawled for the nearest shadows.

He was still crawling when he heard sirens.

Sin came up for air four trucks over and started walking. He dodged behind the diner, behind the dumpster, thought about going back inside but no, he had to get outside the perimeter now, before the cops had a chance to set up.

He walked briskly out to the frontage road, across it and into the ditch. Once he was in the ditch, he ran a loop around the outside of the parking lot towards the hotel. He didn't stop until he got back to el Viejo's minivan.

He leaned up against it, cold metal on his

back, and looked at his left hand. His little finger was turning blue at the tip, purple up where it met his palm. There was no way to shoot a .45 with your little finger and not fuck your wrist up pretty good. But still, Sin felt a happy tremble beneath his eyes and his hands and his shoulders shook with joy. "Holy fuck," he thought. "I just murdered a trained international mercenary shooting a custom 1911 upside down with my off hand." He struggled to suppress the next thought, but there it was. "I am fucking awesome."

Such a dumb thought to have.

He looked up. Five hundred yards across the lot, the police were convening over the body of the fallen mercenary. Spiraling blue lights in the air, flashlights cutting across the pavement and then being swallowed up by the space in between the semis.

Sin reached into his pocket for the keys to the van, not thinking, not listening, not living in Condition Yellow. Even the sound of the gun tapping on the side of the minivan was white noise. Then Sin heard it again and his insides went to ice.

"Knock knock, Shelia. Get in the van like a good boy and get us the fuck out of here." Sin looked back and the man said, "Don't look. Unlock the van," but Sin saw he had a wicked Steyr AUG bullpup assault rifle. The man held it pulled back tight against his shoulder, resting his cheek on it, and he had it trained on Sin – center mass. Finger was off the trigger though. For now.

Sin hit the button and the van beeped. Quickly, the man slid the door open and got into the second row of seats. "Get in and drive," he said.

Sin looked at the lights and the sirens. He didn't seem to have a ton of options right then. He got in, started the engine, and wheeled onto the road. He felt the man's hand snake around and remove the 1911 from his holster.

"What's your name?" the man said as he slipped the 1911 into his waistbelt, Mexican carry.

Sin looked up at the rearview mirror, took a closer look at the man in the backseat. He was younger than Sin'd thought, but he'd spent his whole life running around the world, finding fights he could fight, and he looked old now. He kept his hair short and his beard long. He had on a black rag crewneck sweater with a long tail and lightweight tactical pants. He still had the rifle up against his cheek. "Name. Now," he demanded again.

"Sin."

"That American air force? Like Maverick?"

"It's just my name."

"Fucking bag men. You're all alike. Where's the money?"

"You're not going to believe this," Sin said. "I don't have it. You got the wrong guy."

"God, you're a dumb one. If you don't have the money, I got no reason to keep you alive."

"You're kind of going to kill me anyway, right?"

"I can kill you with my gun or my knife. Your choice, Sheila."

Sin said nothing.

"That man back there, I served with him for years. Ten years."

Sin said nothing to that, either.

They were coming up on the on ramp to the highway. The man said, "Take it south," and waited for Sin to turn the wheels on the minivan and accelerate into traffic before he spoke again.

"This whole thing a set up?"

"What whole thing?"

"Oh fuck off with this," the man spat. "Answer the question."

Sin had to think. What would a detective say? Finally he said, "Yeah, I guess it was."

"Who?"

"Diablo?"

"I'm going to shoot you in the fucking head if you lie to me again."

Sin looked back at the weapon and said, "With a Steyr AUG bullpup assault rifle? Please. Bullet would go through the windshield into the next car. You switched to the 1911, maybe."

The man's eyes narrowed. "You said you weren't military."

"Said I wasn't air force."

"Why does Diablo care if we get paid? He doesn't even know our names."

Sin swore internally, trying to figure out what was going on. But he felt proud, too. He'd gotten some information out of the man.

"Next exit, turn," the man said again.

The exit led straight off into nowhere, a stretch of asphalt, a sign saying a town Sin'd never heard of was twenty-five miles away. It wasn't but eight o'clock yet, and the stars were just starting to push out past the sheer film of light that still glowed on the western horizon.

Sin took a deep breath. "Diablo, he told me he didn't want Americans hit through his operation. He seemed real mad. Said it could bring down the whole thing, border patrol found out."

"You seem to know a lot about my work for a contractor, boy. You sure you don't have a box of my money back there?"

Sin said nothing and the man nodded and said, "All right then. Bag man."

For nearly an hour then, there was only quiet air and the sound of tires on a road that could have been any of the roads that Sin'd lived his life on, all two-lane, all blacktop worn to gray, all dirt shouldered, all pointed square at the edge of a wide flat world.

Finally, the man clicked his tongue twice and said, "See the sign?"

Sin did. It read Lucky U and it was pink and pocked and it marked a single-story whitewalled motel.

"Pull in, stop the vehicle. Far corner."

The Lucky U was the only building Sin could see all the way out to the horizon and it had gravel for a parking lot and his tires crunched as he pulled into the dark corner next to a sad oak someone'd planted but didn't have the heart to water.

The only other cars in the lot were midlevel sedans, new Fords and used BMWs. But there were a few girls sitting on lawn chairs out front of the lobby, each of them about twenty and wearing a tube top and teased hair from some lost decade.

As the minivan slowed, the girls stopped their gossip and stood and then, one by one, disappeared into the motel, leaving a narrow beam of light spreading into the lot as the door swung behind them.

After a second or two, the door latched back shut and the parking lot was pitch dark again.

"This a place with girls?"

"'This a place with girls?'" The man sneered. "Jesus Christ. Get out, cross your hands in front of your body, place your palms on your shoulders. Do it now."

Slowly Sin exited the car.

"Now go around and with your left hand, open your hatch."

Sin scanned the motel. If any of the girls was still watching, they'd darkened their doors. Behind a couple of curtains, he could see shadows moving. He reached down and pulled up on the latch, swung the back of the minivan open wide.

The man looked over Sin's shoulder into the trunk. The blankets had been carefully arranged, but he could see the outline of a box there on the floor of the van.

"Open it," he said.

Sin slowly reached in and slid the blankets away. He'd flipped the latch and started to open the lid when he felt the bullpup in his back.

"Good boy. Step back," the man said. "Arms crossed, hands on shoulders."

Sin did as he was told and the man took his place, slowly opening the box, looking for money, looking, looking, finally seeing not money, but worn wood and polished bolt action.

The M40.

He wheeled around as fast as he could, saying, "Who the fuck…" trying to bring the bullpup on Sin's body but Sin was lower than he'd been before and was pushing up on the barrel with one hand, trying to put the man's eyes out with the other.

The mercenary was fast though, and there wasn't a lot he hadn't seen. He relaxed, let Sin keep pushing the barrel up, and brought the butt around, crack, into Sin's jaw.

As Sin pulled his right hand back towards his face, the man stomped down his shin, scraping through his jeans at flesh, landing the sole of his boot bang on top of Sin's foot.

Sin tried to keep his left hand on the rifle as he fell, held on to it so hard, clung like a toddler clings to a mother's leg. With his right, he reached out and grabbed the man's waistbelt.

The man shook the rifle back and forth and

skinny Sin shook back and forth with it, the soles of his shoes skittering across the pebbled parking lot. The man swung hard and Sin's feet whipped around and he banged sideways into the van, his body folding around its corner, his ribcage flexing beneath the fender as he slipped towards the ground.

The man held the bullpup to Sin's head and said, "Who are you working for?"

Sin was face down on the ground and blood seeped from his mouth black into the gravel. Out the corner of his eye, he could see the tires of the minivan and they were just like the tires of a work truck a decade ago when he'd been lying beaten on the dirt, waiting for a bigger, stronger guy to come kill him. But this time, no one was going to show up to save Sin.

He said to the earth below, "Where'd you bury him?"

"Bury who?"

"My uncle."

"Your uncle. Oh hell. The fat man? In the wind, Shelia. We burned him outside the bloody staging site."

Sin thought how guns are tools. For this.

His right hand came out from the shadows beneath his left armpit and it had the 1911 in it and the mercenary tried to figure out when Sin'd taken it and in that split second of incomprehension Sin shot him in the hand and then twice in the body and then once in the head. The man died with his index finger where he'd been trained to keep it. On the side, outside the trigger guard until you're on target and ready to fire.

Sin reached up, grabbed the fender of the minivan, pulled himself back onto his feet. He couldn't stand up all the way, his ribs hurt so bad and his bad knee was seizing up and his left hand had turned totally blue.

There was blood sprayed across the minivan where the man had fallen. Sin thought about reaching down to look for a pulse, but that seemed stupid, given the guy was missing half his head.

Sin lifted his t-shirt up so it covered his face all the way up to his eyes. Then he turned and looked at the motel. Every light had been turned off and there was no motion behind the curtains, not that he could see, anyway.

He climbed back into the minivan and left a ten-foot spray of pebbles behind him.

Sin parked the minivan two miles from the staging site, took off his shoes, and jogged in. It'd been twenty-six hours since he'd slept, but his body just kept going. One foot in front of the other, his feet floating over sand and rock. Running barefoot through the desert.

Like the Apaches used to train their kids.

The sun came up as he ran and it was a wonderful thing. White-blue rims appeared over the horizon and then it was like the mesas had been given kings' crowns made of the yellow light that came shooting off them, firing bang in all directions.

Sin dropped about three hundred yards out and pulled the binoculars out of the go-bag. Nothing. Not just no movement, but nothing. Somebody had come in and cleaned the site. The trailers, gone. The bodies, gone. The cans and the tins, gone and gone.

It was just a hundred square feet of dry dirt in

between a couple mesas.

Sin surveilled the site for an hour before edging his way in.

Somewhere out towards where the land bottomed out there was a wide, flat outcropping of rock spreading up out of the dirt and on the rock there was a charring.

Whatever ash there was had been taken by the wind, but clinging in the creosote there were bits of cloth. A hard throw away, Sin found a blackened turquoise belt buckle.

Sin walked along the outcropping until he found an edge where the rock receded deep back into the earth. He unwrapped el Viejo's cane from the straps of the go-bag, lifted it high and stabbed it into the ground. He had to pick it up and bring it back down, over and over, breaking up hardpack until the cane found purchase beneath and finally stood upright in the desert.

Sin cupped his hands and packed dirt into the hole and then watched as the winds surrounded the cane with a gentle layer of shifting dust.

Sin unclipped his pistol, set it on the ground,

laid down flat on the rock, and folded his arms across his chest. He tried to imagine himself lying forever in the desert, watching that same sky for all eternity. He watched the clouds and the sun moving through them, and he felt the wash of warming breezes carrying away the sweet scent of night blooming cereus.

It wasn't so bad.

In fact, it was as perfect a grave as any warrior could ever wish.

After a time Sin rose and collected his weapon and walked away. Wasn't 'til he was back to the van he started to cry.

CHAPTER EIGHT: SALIDA, 2008

To the southwest there was a range of fourteeners. Up there the glaciers carved swaths down through the loose gray rock and ended just short of treeline, where a thin band of boulders and moss separated them from the beginnings of the low scrub and the tall pine.

Down in the valley the evergreens and the aspens stood four and five feet apart and the soil in between teemed full of shaded undergrowth, trees felled by beetlekill, wet rocks covered with blue-green moss.

A man walked out of the trees into a clearing, not really looking where he was going, staring into a brown plastic box. He was in his late fifties and he was so thin Sin, at first, mistook him for an aspen.

The man looked up and when he saw the minivan he lifted the box above his head, waving it in triumph. "En svart bjorn!" he shouted.

El Viejo smiled, chortled and called out the window of the minivan, "Congratulations, amigo!"

Sin and el Viejo almost never flew anywhere; it was too big a pain in the ass to check their guns. They'd driven all the way up from Arizona to this place in the southern Colorado mountains. It had taken them twelve hours, the last one on a winding dirt road with a sheer drop on their left side. The road hadn't been cut into the side of the mountains with a minivan in mind, that was for sure.

The thin man started walking up the slope to where they'd parked, still waving the brown box over his head. Sin looked at him, not concerned exactly, but unwilling to lose visual contact until he knew what exactly what was in the box.

El Viejo, as always, could read his mind. "It's a nature camera. They hang it on the trees while they are away to see what wildlife might be prowling the valley in their absence."

Sin nodded. "He seems pretty happy."

"He photographed a bear. Wouldn't you be?"

"That's Petr, right?"

"It is."

"Thought you said he was stone cold Viking killer."

"No, I said Petr was Swedish intelligence, Sin. Not everyone who works in MLE pulls triggers for a living. I believe he analyzed satellite imagery."

"Whatever," Sin said, because that was what he always said when he wasn't saying nothing.

El Viejo reached back behind the drivers seat and picked up his cane. He opened the door, planted the cane on the dirt and pushed hard, leveraging himself out of the minivan just in time to greet Petr. The two men were equally tall, but el Viejo was at least a hundred pounds heavier. Petr clapped him hard on the shoulders and el Viejo said, "My friend, my friend."

And then there she was, twenty yards away, up on the deck of the cabin.

If she didn't have the plastic tube pumping little bursts of oxygen into her nose, she would've been about the most beautiful woman Sin'd ever seen. She had long gray hair that the wind picked up and twisted, holding it high so the mountain sun could play hide and seek with you, shimmering in between the strands. She was an old woman and her skin showed it, but her eyes were so bright and hard that they sparkled like stars magically visible in daytime skies.

She stood on the deck of the cabin, very short but also very straight, one hand on the railing and the other pointing directly at Sin in the passenger seat of the minivan. "So," she called out, her voice echoing off the valley walls, "this is the boy."

And el Viejo rumbled in that giant baritone of his, "Sin, get out of the car. I would like you to meet Special Agent Catrina Limon, la Calavera."

Sin gave a little nod through the windshield

and the beautiful old woman smiled back, her eyes tearing up in the Rocky Mountain wind.

Sin got out of the minivan. He grabbed their two oversized duffels and the go-bag with the .357 in it. He slung them over his shoulder and walked after el Viejo and Petr, who'd already started the gentle climb to the cabin.

When Sin got up the steps, the woman wrapped her arms around him and even kissed his cheek. And then she took hold of his right hand in hers and he was surprised by how firm her grasp was. She held Sin's hand up and said, "And this must be your older sister."

Sin looked at the tattoo that covered the back of his hand. On it stood a little girl in a flannel nightgown, thick red curls piled on top of her head. Her big, believing eyes looked up his forearm through a dark woods, all the way to his elbow where a decaying purple house waited.

Sin looked over at el Viejo, but the man's eyes gave him nothing. They seemed blank and even uncertain.

La Calavera said, "Oh, I have heard much

about you, young Sin. In fact, I know more about you than you know about yourself."

There they were, all together. Four people at the base of a mountain none of them were prepared to climb.

The cabin had running water from a well, solar panels, and enough food that if the zombie apocalypse began, the four of them could've hidden out there a few months. They had some weapons, could've hunted if they had to, but Sin couldn't imagine any of those three old people chasing deer through the pines.

Sin flashed back to his days in Wyoming, watching his dad pop bucks from the back of the pickup. That man had died in a car accident a couple years back. There'd been no drinking or racing or tragic backstory. Just two strangers used to driving their trucks on long stretches of two-lane blacktop without another vehicle for miles around until, suddenly, both trucks were in exactly the same place at exactly the same time. Sin had gone home for the funeral, but mostly he just wanted to see Nicki, his big sister, the only girl he'd ever dreamed about.

Sin sat on the deck by himself for awhile, watching the sun go down, taking deep breaths of piney air, peering into the trees, wondering if the bear was nearby.

El Viejo and la Calavera busied themselves wrapping trout in tin foil and sliding them into the fire in the clay chiminea. Petr boiled hot chocolate and mixed it with peppermint schnapps. He asked el Viejo something in Swedish, which Sin interpreted as, "Is the boy old enough to drink liquor?" And the old man shrugged, which Sin interpreted as, "No, but the hell with it."

La Calavera took her Sierra cup from Petr and settled in a lawn chair next to Sin. The metal of the cup was warm with the hot chocolate inside it, and she wrapped one set of boney fingers around it comfortably. With the other hand, she lowered her oxygen tank onto the ground beside her. She leaned back in her chair. "So your uncle tells me he adopted you?"

Sin half-nodded. "Sort of. I mean, my mom

and dad were still my mom and dad. But Harrison had to raise me."

"Why?"

"Things going on where I was born. Couldn't really deal. Got in some trouble I couldn't get out of."

"What kind of trouble?"

"Seemed real bad at the time. But some of the things me and el Viejo have done the past few years, it wasn't that bad. But I couldn't go to my dad. My mom, even. Maybe I could've, but I didn't. El Viejo came up and sort of kidnapped me. The first day, he took me out to the desert and made me run around barefoot for four hours like I was a little Indian brave kid. But then he'd let me shoot his guns and I liked that. I loved it. I love shooting guns." Sin took another drink. The schnapps cleared out his sinuses and the peppermint made warm wonderful combinations with the scent of the evergreens. He said, "I guess you've seen some fucked up stuff, too, huh?"

She nodded. "I had a good run. I wouldn't have left the ATF except…" She waved elegant, long, old-lady fingers over her oxygen line. "I hear you lost your father?"

Sin studied the trees, his cup, his ink, anything to not make eye contact. "Yeah."

"Must have been hard for you."

Sin shrugged, said, "It was, but it wasn't."

She nodded sagely and followed Sin's eyes off the deck into the forest. Fifty yards deep, there was a squirrel sitting on a fallen pine, using the beetlekill as cover, poking his little head up to look at the mammals up on the cabin deck. "Do you see it?" she whispered.

He nodded.

"Not one person in a hundred would see an animal that small at this distance."

Sin said, "Thought you meant the bobcat."

La Calavera's eyes flashed back out into the forest and she squinted. Sin was right. Behind the squirrel, there was a tuft of ears and a tensing of muscles, a spreading of claws finding purchase on gray rock.

She shook her head and whispered, "El Viejo was right. You're very special, Sin."

At which point, the old man himself swung

open the screen door of the cabin, plates in hand, voice like thunder ricocheting off the valley walls, "My compadres, allow me to announce the readiness of our feast." When the two of them looked back, both the squirrel and the bobcat were gone. Sin and la Calavera simultaneously sighed. El Viejo looked back and forth between them, perplexed. "What have I done now?" he asked and they laughed in response.

He set plates full of trout, corn and pico de gallo on their laps. He looked up at the sky and squinted, holding up two meaty fingers, judging the distance between the sun and the horizon. "We'd best dig in. The sun goes down quickly when you're in a valley," he said.

La Calavera nodded, "But the stars, they will shine so bright."

Petr followed el Viejo out with glasses of white wine and the four of them sat in a circle on the deck.

A breeze came from the forest and lifted Petr's napkin off his lap, pinning it to the railing. While he went to retrieve it, el Viejo said, "Caddo legends tell us sudden winds are the spirits of the dead. The chiefs would gather in a grass house with an open door facing the rising sun. There, they would sing, calling the dead to come home and live again. But many years ago, when no one was watching, Coyote closed the door to the chiefs' house. And so our dead are left to wander the earth as little winds, making mischief until eventually they find the road that leads to the spirit land."

At this, la Calavera laughed bitterly. "No matter what you think is going on, there's almost always some goddamn dead person pulling the strings."

El Viejo nodded. "Cherchez la dead. Isn't that what we used to say, la Calavera? Cityfolk cherchez la femme. In the desert, we cherchez la dead."

She raised her sierra cup in the air and el Viejo followed. Together they toasted, "Cherchez la dead."

Petr smiled and he lifted his cup as well and cheered, "Serge the deep!" And he said it so enthusiastically and happily that they all cheered, raised their glasses and drank again.

There was a stillness that followed, and in it

la Calavera eyed Sin. "What about you, son?" she asked. "Are you old enough to have regrets?"

They all turned to him, but Sin didn't look into any of their eyes. He peered off the deck and saw that now the forest things were shadowed and beyond even his vision. He took a little sip of his white wine, just to wet his lips, and said, "I wouldn't say I have regrets, but I guess I have questions."

"Questions? Oh dear boy." She smiled and looked at Petr, and then el Viejo, and then back to Sin. "You are just going to have to get used to living with them."

Sin's eyes flicked from the forest over to where el Viejo sat leaning heavily forward, elbows on his knees. It took some time for Sin to adjust to the firelight, but when he did all he saw was an old man staring at an older woman.

El Viejo said, "Have you had your questions answered, la Calavera?"

She didn't say anything at first. She turned her eyes away from el Viejo and stared into the chiminea for a long time. Finally she looked back up at him. And she said, "Cherchez la dead."

Sin lifted his cup into the air again and began to toast, "Cherchez…" But no one joined him. He shrugged, lifted the liquor to his lips, and drank alone.

CHAPTER NINE: ARIZONA, 2011

Sin woke up in the minivan about three in the afternoon at a rest stop off the highway, and only because it was hot and he was dripping sweat, like a dog dying in an overheated car.

Three hours of sleep in an exposed location.

Jesus Christ.

What was he going to do without his el Viejo?

He stared out the windows, tried to think of a

way to tell his mom her brother was a skeleton. Gone forever. Never coming back.

And he had to tell la Calavera and Petr, too, tell them that some mercenaries knocked off el Viejo for what? The old man wasn't doing any work. Wasn't chasing anyone or making any enemies. Had to be revenge for something he did way back when. Some criminal he'd jailed or ghosted or offended somehow.

And he had to tell Nicki.

The last time Sin'd seen his sister he'd put her on a plane bound for places unknown. Nicki had four million in her purse she could use to find her way.

What did Sin have? Just guns.

To Sin it seemed like everything had returned to how it was a dozen years ago, back when Nicki went to New York. She was off living life while he was fighting through his days, missing her like crazy, not sure how to tell her how much he needed her to come home.

Nicki was a selfish bitch and it just made Sin love her more.

He got out of the minivan. Out here, the oaks didn't dare grow. It was just dirt on the verge of becoming dust. Sometimes a cactus or a patch of sage grass.

Sin walked around to the shoulder of the road and sat in the shade of the minivan, ass on the pavement. He sent a text. Two minutes later, his cell rang, an international number popping up on the caller ID.

He answered, "Hey, Nick."

"Hey, bro. You ok?"

"Where are you?"

"Better if you don't know. You're planning a trip, fly into London, I could talk you in?"

"Yeah Nick, you gotta cut it out. I need to tell you something."

She paused and then said, "What's up? You in trouble?"

"No, it's Uncle Harrison."

"Yeah?"

"Uncle Harrison, he's gone, he's dead."

Nicki made a sharp little whimpering sound like she'd been pinched. Then, "Oh, Sin. God. Oh,

I'm sorry."

"Yeah."

"Was it, like, a heart attack? Or kidneys? Mom said with the diabetes, it was going to be the kidneys."

"No. He was, it was, like a criminal thing, someone shot him, some reason."

"Oh shit." He heard her breath catch.

"Yeah."

"Now?"

"Yeah."

"He's like seventy."

"I..." Sin started to cry. He tried to squint, pass it off like it was the sun, but it wasn't. The muscles in his stomach started heaving and his ribs hurt, he was shaking so bad, and they hurt where the merc had folded him across the fender of his own minivan and his left wrist had stopped being blue and now it was just purple and almost black.

She said, "Sin..."

But he couldn't be stopped. "You know, Nick, revenge, that's why he came, got me in the first place. Stop me from killing those motherfuckers." Sin stopped to spit on the side of the road. A truck flew by too fast and Sin flipped it off as it disappeared towards the horizon. It made him feel better. He swallowed and went on. "Revenge is what I wanted and he was who stopped me from living that way. But that's why he's dead, someone with some old score they hired someone to even up. But Nick, you wouldn't believe it. They weren't even sure what it was anymore. They looked at me, couldn't even tell me why. It was like if I went to kill those three cowboy hick fuckers now, they wouldn't even know who I was, I bet. It was like that. Some old bullshit no one even cares about anymore."

"Well, two."

"No, there was three."

"Yeah, Sin, I know. But the one, he died in an accident the same day Uncle Harrison came to get you. The one used to play JV football when John was graduating. Steve or Scott or something. Something Limon."

And suddenly Sin wasn't standing by the edge of the road at all. He was floating somewhere else entirely, his skin tingling, his ears not even connected to his body as Nicki continued to talk. The walls had been knocked off the world, the horizons raced away. There was nothing to hold him. No container. Maybe never had been.

"He had an accident in his barn that same day, fell off their hay loft, bounced his head off the windshield of their truck. Seems like maybe god got your revenge for you, huh."

Sin said, "Wasn't god."

"Huh?"

"Nothing."

"You OK? Those guys who killed Uncle Harrison, don't do anything stupid, Sin."

"Nick, I gotta go."

Sin hung up without waiting for his sister to say goodbye.

He stood by the side of the road, feeling the wind pick up dust and throw it against his face. He squeezed his phone in his fist, gritted his teeth, let out a sound that should've been a roar but wasn't quite.

He pulled the 1911 right there on the side of the road, cars whipping by, dropped the clip and counted rounds. Then he tapped his phone and found the fastest route to Green Valley.

It'd be almost sunset when he got there.

Perfect.

The first thing la Calavera heard was a whisper. "How could you think I wouldn't figure it out?"

There was a pause and then she took a half breath and said, "Hello, Sin."

Sin was crouched down low on the floor behind the wheelchair. He pushed the barrel of the 1911 into the base of her fragile old neck, just so she knew it was there, and then he swiftly pulled it back again, keeping it out of her elbow's reach. He said again, "How?"

"Actually." Breathe. "I'm stunned." Breathe. "It took you." Breathe. "So long." Go on and take a breath, you old bitch. You don't have many more left.

"You still got that snubby under your blanket?"

She nodded.

"Hands out, palms up."

And she nodded again.

Outside the sliding doors, past the ten-foot square patio and the row of desert flowers and over the adobe fence, the sun was almost down. Sin looked out at the horizon. Maybe fifteen minutes until dark.

"Petr?" she asked.

"Tied up in the bedroom. Your alarm sucks."

"Hm," she smiled. "You are more like me than your uncle, you know."

"Fuck you to hell," Sin said. He slid left from behind the wheelchair, right hand keeping the 1911 pointed at Catrina, left hand in a fist out of the way against his chest, careful not to cross his feet. He stopped in a full crouch just behind her ear. If she turned her scrawny fucking skull way to the left, she could just barely see him squatting there.

He said, "That's why my uncle took you under his wing when you came here. He saw your file, realized he'd ghosted your grandson, had to be your best friend out of guilt or something."

"I suppose."

"How long was it, you knew it too?"

Her bony shoulders moved up and down, a tiny shrug. Even thinking about the past was hard. "A year. I think. He wanted to tell me. Eventually, it slipped out. In pieces. Over drinks. In trucks, on stakeouts. I have lived with this a long time."

"Why now?"

The old lady spoke so slowly. But Sin let her finish. He could give her that. She said, "El Viejo risked everything for a boy he barely knew. There is a boy I love, too. A boy I once carried inside me. Just like your mother carried you. And he had a son, a son he loved, he did." She let out a breath that wasn't breath, it was a sigh. "I'd made a promise to my boy. I couldn't die before it was kept."

"And then you sent me to take out the men you sent to kill my uncle."

"I couldn't have them traipsing around the border, bragging about their assassination of a national hero."

"I should've known. How many other people in the world have the connections it'd take to run

Aussie mercs through cartel slave trails?"

"Not many."

"And you told them to wait for delivery of the cash in Yuma. Sitting ducks, waiting to get paid."

"They're dead?"

"Dead."

"Oh Sin. Trained soldiers, cartel outlaws – you wiped them all out, cleared the desert in three days."

"I could've been killed."

The old lady looked up at him, eyes burning red. "Lets not forget, you murdered my grandson."

"I was twelve."

"He was seventeen."

The shadows crawling into the room had finally reached the far edge of the floor. Sin stood up, brought his hands together in front of his heart, pushed the weapon out, focused on the front sight, and lined it up on la Calavera's head. This close, the bullet would go right through her, ricochet off the tile into the wall. Her brains and bits of her skull would splatter over the glass door. One bang. This hour? In a retirement community? The neighbors wouldn't even have their hearing aids on. Petr could weasel out of his ropes and spend all night mopping up his wife.

Sin said, "Last words, la Calavera."

She nodded. "I remember one day, after my first husband left me, before I met Petr, my son brought his family to the cabin. Scott was a baby then, just one or two. They took him off into the wildflowers and set out a yellow blanket. They sat out there together, reading a story. I remember. I stood on the deck watching my son and his wife and my grandson together, the way a family is meant to be. It was so perfect. And I remember thinking, it's just like a picture. Like a picture."

She closed her eyes, holding that memory, floating inside it, and as she did, her wrinkled face smoothed in the flat dusk light and her breath sounded even at last.

The next noise she heard was the click of the latch as the front door closed behind Sin.

She opened her eyes and smiled, not because she was alive, but that anyone's footsteps could be so soft. "That young man is simply a ninja," she thought. And then she turned her eyes out the window to look for the sunset.

It wouldn't be long now.

She waited until the light was gone and then moved her boney hands to the cold metal rims on the side of her wheelchair. She pushed as hard as her body would allow, rolling down the hall so she could go untie her husband.

It'd been days since Sin'd seen Sindy. When he walked into the tattoo parlor around nine that night, she seemed relieved, maybe even happy to catch sight of him out of the corner of her eye.

"That your man?" said the girl laid out on Sindy's bench, a dragon sketched on her ribcage.

Sindy nodded a little, not too much, trying to keep her hand steady and her eyes on the needle plug plug plugging into the girl's skin. "Something like that," she murmured. Louder, she called out, "Ink or a drink, sailor?"

But Sin said nothing back. He just stared at Sindy and tried to imagine a life where they got married and had babies, bought a house or whatever.

He couldn't quite get the picture to focus in his mind, so he thought, "Maybe all the planning doesn't matter. Maybe me and Sindy, we could just find a way to help each other through the days. And we'd be together when sunset came and that would be enough."

After a few moments, Sindy looked up from the tattoo she was doing, wondering if Sin was going to answer her question. And seeing him looking back at her she smiled, even though she had a teardrop tattooed on her perfect pink cheek.

Matt Ingwalson *is the author of the Owl & Raccoon series of police procedurals and the upcoming novel* Regret Things. *They're available on Amazon.*

Coming soon: *Sin's sister Nicki ran away to Manhattan at the age of 18. While she was there she lived as an artist, an anarchist, an ad executive, and finally a criminal. Years later, some very bad men come hunting for her. And Sin, el Viejo, and all the other men in Nicki's life find themselves caught up in a revenge saga that will stretch from the sidewalks of Madison Avenue to the reservation lands of New Mexico.* Regret Things, *a new novel about Nicki and Sin, will be out 2014.*

Made in the USA
San Bernardino, CA
04 May 2014